"There's a real world, Erinna,
not just a romantic fantasy."

Erinna was infuriated by John's words.
What did he know about feelings? About
people?

Then her currents of rage mingled with
amazement. For suddenly his head lowered,
and his mouth sought and found hers. It
was a pure, profound physical shock. The
kiss had nothing tentative about it. A long
subtle exploration, it was a positive
statement, not a question.

When at last he drew back, her eyes were
glistening, bright, but bewildered.

"Fantasy, or reality?" he murmured. "Who's
going to say?"

For once in her life Erinna
was speechless. . . .

Rowan Kirby, happily married for eighteen years to an ex-research scientist, has two teenage children and lives near Bristol. With a degree in English, she has spent time teaching English to foreign students and has been involved in adult literacy instruction. She always wanted to write and has had articles published in newspapers and women's magazines.

Books by Rowan Kirby

HARLEQUIN ROMANCE

Only My Dreams

Rowan Kirby

Harlequin Books

TORONTO • NEW YORK • LONDON
AMSTERDAM • PARIS • SYDNEY • HAMBURG
STOCKHOLM • ATHENS • TOKYO • MILAN

Original hardcover edition published in 1988
by Mills & Boon Limited

ISBN 0-373-02960-8

Harlequin Romance first edition February 1989

For Tamsin
– (an original creation,
and now an inspiration)
with my love

CHAPTER ONE

THIS was the coldest January Britain had seen for years. Since the War, some said, or even since records began. Be that as it may, snow and ice were dramatic, with temperatures plummeting well below zero and most of the nation plunged into a state of paralysis.

John Bryce observed all this with his usual detached amusement. In his experience, winters were designed to be cold, just as summers were predictably hot. He might be on home territory now, but he'd been out and about in the world this past decade, sampling a variety of climates and continents. There were many differences between them, but one rule they did share. Unless you were on the equator, seasons changed and became warmer or cooler. Wasn't it possible to be prepared for both?

It seemed to John that these islanders were never ready for extremes in either direction. Every year, without fail, they managed to be outraged and excited by blizzards and blisters alike. Moderation in all things, that was the British mentality.

His colleagues and students, here at the University of Mid-Anglia, were apparently no exception. So, their ordinary campus was suddenly picturesque under fifteen inches of snow, and their lake frozen solid—was that really justification for this juvenile sporting and cavorting John was witnessing now? A crisp Sunday morning, and here he was, trying to jog his daily route round the lake, as he'd continued to do since September, whatever the weather. But today his progress was severely impeded by these hysterical revellers, shrieking as they slithered on and off the ice, giggling as they staggered and wallowed in snowdrifts. Bundled up to the eyes in hats and scarves so that it was a challenge to tell male from female or staff from student, still less pick out individual faces.

He swerved to avoid another group, busy lacing up their skating boots. Time for a touch of the Torvill-and-Deans. At least this lot were behaving with some of the decorum one might expect from members of such an institution.

John flashed them a smile as he jogged by. He knew how exhilarating ice skating could be, once you'd mastered the technique. Where had he learned it? Canada, wasn't it? Yes, he was sure the first time had been in Winnipeg, must be eight or nine years ago now, when one of his fellow lecturers had lent him some skates. He was strong and fit, confident and athletic, and as a kid he'd been an expert roller-skater. So it hadn't taken him many minutes to find his balance and sail out on that glassy surface, relishing the unique sense of freedom and grace, along with the others.

He closed his eyes as he recalled it now—but only for a moment. He had grown beyond such fancies, these days. He jogged to keep his system in trim. Whatever John did, there was good reason. Pure pleasure—he'd call it self-indulgence now—was for the young and hedonistic, not for the likes of Dr Bryce, hard-headed academic, master of his subject and of himself, respected Visiting Fellow in Literature at this highly regarded seat of learning. Then there were his other, less public achievements, but those had nothing to do with what went on here, even if he couldn't always banish them from his inner self while...

Damn! He must watch where he was stepping, or he'd end up with soggy running shoes. Keep to the path, which had been cleared, and...

Splat! The hefty snowball caught him square in the face. Powder-soft, yet damply chill, stinging his skin, knocking his breath away. He reeled, skidded, clutched at air—but then he was down, sprawling in the slush, undignified and enraged.

'What the *hell*?' He was on his feet again at once, glaring round. 'Who threw that?'

No one claimed responsibility, but no one was beating a hasty retreat either. He dusted snow from his tracksuit. Some of it was trickling unpleasantly down his neck. He glowered round again; surely someone must be slinking guiltily away, or worse, sniggering from a safe distance?

He shrugged. What the hell did it matter, anyway? He was above worrying about such trivialities, or at least, showing he was worried. He paced up and down a couple of times on the spot, ready to jog on.

'Dr Bryce!'

He swung round. Now a figure was detaching itself from the crowds and sauntering towards him—evidently unperturbed, hands in pockets, scarlet wellingtons carving a straight track through the snow.

'Dr Bryce, are you OK?'

John's frown deepened. No problem defining the gender or status of this customer. She wouldn't be one to bother with hats, and her flaming auburn mop gleamed, catching reflected glints off sun and snow. As she drew nearer, her features became clear—but he knew them before he saw them. He knew the amazing green eyes, creamy translucent skin, freckled nose and cheeks, wide mouth. Initial impressions labelled her gamine, even elfin—but look again, and she was rounded, curving in all the desirable places. Rather more curvaceous than average, as John had noted, first encountering her about four months ago—and gone on noting ever since, with a kind of reluctant satisfaction.

Erinna Casey was one of his top Finalists. As brilliant as she was erratic; as infuriating as she was beguiling. Thoroughbred Irish, a Celt from accent to name, from complexion to personality. So what was she doing here, in the English department of this English University?

He had no intention of asking her. He kept his distance from everyone, especially students, even more especially his own undergraduates. They were here to learn, and he was here to teach, and that was how it had better stay. Too bad if they teased and tempted him, used his first name, tried to involve him in their social and extramural activities. After all, they implied, he was—what? Only eleven, twelve years older than they were? And this was the age, and the heart, of democracy, wasn't it?

But he remained aloof, minding his own business and signalling them to mind theirs. He was expert at the job and that had to be enough. If they were after personal contact with their tutors and professors, there were plenty only too willing to provide it. John Bryce was not among them.

'Dr Bryce, you're not hurt, are you?'

She'd reached him now; it was too late to ignore her, so he stood his ground and surveyed her coldly—in more ways than one.

'I'm sorry. It was an accident. Or rather, a miscalculation.'

She had this low, lyrical voice, one of her most striking qualities. However volatile she became—and he'd seen her worked up, more than once, discussing some poem or a finer point in Shakespeare—she kept her tone modulated. The words flowed fast, articulate, yes—but always controlled.

'Her voice was ever soft, gentle and low, an excellent thing in woman...' Now, who was it said that, and in which play? King Lear, of course, lamenting the death of his beloved Cordelia; a poignant scene, in which...

'*Dr Bryce!*' She waited, patiently, until she had his full attention. 'You're all right, are you?'

'I think so, Erinna.' His eyes were sharp on her face. 'No thanks to you.'

His own voice was deep and rich, with suggestions of a transatlantic drawl—Canadian, perhaps, or was it American? She was never quite sure.

'I'm really sorry. It wasn't aimed at you, honestly.'

'You don't say.' He was sceptical, but those green eyes were direct and lucid, unflinching from his, and her expression solemn.

'Didn't you see Dave Curtis? He was on the lake, just behind you. I thought you'd be well out of the way by the time the...'

'No, I didn't. I didn't *see* anyone. I was fully occupied, avoiding fatal collisions on the path.'

'Well, he was there,' she assured him, 'and we thought we'd timed it exactly right. But we obviously missed him by several feet.'

John considered all this, keeping his expression bland, a match for hers. 'It seems your aim leaves a lot more room for improvement than your work. Thank God I'll never have to confront you on a cricket pitch.'

'How do you know? I may not be much of a bowler, but I could be a genius batsman!'

John allowed himself a fleeting grin. 'Don't you mean batsperson?'

'If you insist.' She took her hands from her pockets; they were encased in gaudy striped mittens. 'I'm not fussy about that. Life's too short. *I* know I'm a woman. I don't need semantics to reinforce it.'

She smiled then, and it was a lamp, glowing on each part of her face, even, he could swear, adding highlights to the remarkable hair.

'Anyway,' she went on, still smiling, 'I do apologise about that. I hope you won't register your indignation by marking my latest essay down?'

Her smile was infectious, but he resisted. In fact, he drew himself up to his considerable height and mustered every ounce of dignity. If it emerged as pomposity, that was too bad.

'I accept your apology for laying me low, Erinna, but I take even less kindly to the suggestion that I might be open to such—subjective criteria in assessing my students' work.'

Her smile faded, but she was undaunted. 'I beg your pardon again, then.'

'Granted,' he said stiffly.

There was a slight pause, and then her smile reappeared.

'You look cold, Dr Bryce. Your knees and—er—your trousers are wet. You must have landed sitting down,' she added, graphically. 'I'm surprised you don't wear a coat. You must be the only person out here who isn't.'

'I wear two tracksuits. Usually,' he pointed out sternly, 'I keep on the move. Given the choice, I don't grovel in the slush, or hang about chatting.'

Erinna inclined her bright head. 'Sorry yet again. I stand corrected, on all counts. I humble myself before you, Dr Bryce.'

He studied her. He had rarely seen anyone who looked less humble, but he let it pass. She was right, he *was* growing chilly, definitely a very bad idea.

'Ten o'clock tomorrow morning, I believe? Our next tutorial?'

'That's right. I'll have my Wordsworth notes ready.'

'"Intimations of Immortality", wasn't it?'

'Certainly was. Becky was writing the essay, but I said I'd get a few thoughts together, too. Since that's one of my special papers, we decided we should cover as much ground as possible.'

'Absolutely.' On safe territory, he softened, and it was her turn to respond to the sudden warmth of his smile—his real smile, illuminating the stony caution of his face. Erinna had watched this abrupt change before, of course, in four months' regular contact, but it never failed to affect her. 'The Romantic Poets,' he was musing now. 'Should be on everyone's special paper, in my opinion.'

'Mine too, but then, we know that.' She chuckled. There was no secret about the fact that Erinna Casey was a Romantic, through and through. In life, as in literature, her creed and her character. 'Actually,' she went on, 'Becky wasn't feeling very well yesterday. Sort of limp, and hot-and-cold, you know. I haven't seen her today, but she certainly isn't out here, so I hope she isn't sickening for anything.'

'Oh, dear.' His concern was quite genuine. 'Did she go to the nurse?'

'I don't know. She's not on my block—I mean, I don't see her all that often. I must remember to ask one of the others.'

Reminded of the others, she glanced over her shoulder. Sure enough, her companions had drifted in their direction, curious about this confrontation, wondering how Erinna had coped with the intimidating Dr Bryce after that superb swipe with the snowball...not that she'd done it on purpose, of course. Or had she? They couldn't be quite sure, even now, and she was notoriously enigmatic.

She seemed to be managing fine without them, returning their cheery waves, poised and upfront as ever. They left her to it. If anyone could deal with such a situation, Erinna could, with her Tipperary charm.

'Well, I dare say we'd survive without her,' John was remarking, back to his unbending self now—wrapping his arms about his body, which was starting to shiver.

'Of course we would.' It was Erinna who registered concern this time. 'Get on with you now, you'll catch your death, and I can't have *that* on my conscience!' She turned and set off away from him, with a quick wave. Before he could react, she was turning back. 'Want me to come and fix you a hot toddy? Whisky and milk, that's what my grandma used to swear by. After all, it's my fault if you're...'

John winced, and she wondered whether it was the idea of whisky and milk, or the prospect of her company. Then she wondered why she cared, either way.

'No, thanks, Erinna. I have my own recipes for cockle-warming concoctions. Thanks all the same.'

On this cryptic note he was off along the path. Erinna watched him for a few seconds as he jogged into the distance, then she trudged back to her expectant friends.

'Hey, what's all this I hear, about you taking pot-shots at our best lecturer?'

'Yeah, is it true he actually grovelled in the snow?'

'Did you mean to hit him, or was it really an accident?'

Erinna's smile did not waver, but inwardly she flinched. This must be the fifth time she'd fielded the story since it had got out at lunch. She hadn't particularly wanted to pursue it the first time; this evening, propping up the Union bar with a few of her friends, she felt allergic to the whole business.

She lobbed their questions expertly back. 'Bryce may be our best lecturer. He's also our most arrogant. It won't do him any harm to have a bit of a grovel.'

'Oh, Erinna!' Clare was even more breathlessly pink than usual. 'You're cruel! He's something else, you know he is. Those incredible eyes, and the voice, and that face...so private...so...'

'Suffering?'

'Lived-in?'

'Experienced?'

Helpful suggestions poured from every side, except Erinna.

'And then there's the body.' Lisa was the sophisticated one. 'He keeps in great shape for a man over thirty,' she mused, lasciviously.

'Not to mention the brain,' Colin pointed out, a little sharply.

'It's all very well for you lot,' Erinna snapped. 'You don't have to have tutorials with him.'

'But his lectures are amazing. That one on Shelley the other day...' Mike blushed, taking refuge behind his glass of lager, but he went on gazing at Erinna. That was nothing new; Mike was generally gazing at Erinna, if she was within sight.

'Sure, I grant you, he gets the message across wonderfully. His work on Shakespeare is acclaimed nationwide. But as a man...'

'Don't you mean worldwide?' Tariq interrupted her. 'Isn't he some kind of media megastar? I mean, even *I've* seen and heard some of his books and programmes, and I'm only a simple physicist.'

'Philistine!' Erinna grinned at him. 'You wouldn't know a line out of *Hamlet* from *Dynasty*!'

He aimed a punch at her, which she ducked. 'Just for that, you can buy me another drink!'

'I'd love to, Tariq, but I'm broke. Living entirely off the whim of my bank manager.'

'Aren't we all?' muttered Lisa.

'It's all right,' Tariq said quickly. 'I was only joking. I've had more than enough already—Monday tomorrow.'

Suddenly, no one was looking at Erinna, not even Mike. They were chatting animatedly, as if to cover an awkwardness. Erinna sighed, sipping her apple juice. It was tactful, the way they protected her when it came to the delicate matter of her position in life, her background, her situation; whatever you called it, things weren't exactly easy.

'Did you go on that march in London last term?' Colin was asking.

'The one about grants? You bet I did! Not that it'll do any good.'

'I don't know any students who haven't got massive overdrafts.'

'Except our Becky.' Lisa was envious. 'She's always loaded.'

'Well, she's an exception; her parents are rolling. Her father's Something in the City,' Clare explained.

'Talking of Becky.' Erinna pushed her way back into the conversation. 'How is she? I heard she was feeling rough, and I haven't seen her since yesterday. She hasn't taken to her bed, has she?'

'Didn't you know?' Clare was always a fund of juicy gossip. 'She was carted off to the sick bay!'

'Why, what's the matter?'

'Glandular fever.'

'Infectious mononucleosis.' Tariq was usually handy with the technicalities.

Erinna was aghast, and not only on Becky's account. 'Oh, God, poor girl! How awful! That can go on for weeks, can't it?'

'It certainly can. She'll be confined to barracks till she's clear, and that could be the rest of the term. In fact, I expect she'll be sent home,' Clare crowed.

'I doubt she'll be allowed to sit her Finals,' Lisa speculated.

Mike's eyes were on Erinna again. 'Don't you share tutorials with her, Erinna? The one with Dr Bryce, isn't it?'

'The very same. Special Papers, Monday morning. And now,' she remarked breezily, before any kind person could do it for her, 'I'll have him all to myself. What a treat!'

'At least you'll get individual attention.' Colin was trying to be encouraging, but Erinna's grunt spoke volumes. Individual attention from John Bryce was the last privilege she needed. In fact, her fists were involuntarily clenching at the mere prospect.

'Some people land all the luck!' Clare moaned. 'You're bound to get that First now. Quite apart from being closeted with...'

Erinna rounded on her. 'That's a stupid thing to say, Clare! It won't make the slightest difference to my degree, or anything else.'

'OK, OK!' Clare fended her off, pouting. Erinna was always forceful, but not often aggressive. 'I take it back! Let's just say I think you're lucky on—other levels!' she simpered.

Erinna subsided, but she was still angry. 'We can agree to differ on that, Clare. But you'd better believe it won't make any odds to my results, whether there are two of us in that study or twelve. He's not going to get any less pompous or opinionated. In fact he'll most likely be worse, without Becky to give us a few laughs.' The more she considered it, the more she dreaded it.

'Come on, Erinna, he can't be *that* bad!' Lisa protested.

'He's all intellect. He has a superb mind, and no soul.'

Mike was fascinated. He had never seen Erinna so flushed, or heard that musical voice so harsh. 'Is that why you chucked the snowball at him? To give him something to feel, instead of just thinking?'

Erinna managed a slight smile. 'I told you, it wasn't deliberate. I was aiming at that slob Dave Curtis and I missed, that's all.'

They seemed prepared to take her word for it, which only proved that you could fool most of the people most of the time. Erinna wasn't fooling herself, of course. She'd hurled the thing on the spur of the moment, unpremeditated, but she'd been in no doubt about her target. Jogging steadily along his regular route, as if it wasn't under inches of snow—not a twitch of excitement or pleasure, not even the tiniest deviation from his schedule. She had been seized by such a surge of illogical irritation, her arm had found a new power and her eye a new aim which she had never achieved before. And very satisfying, too.

'Well, I'm glad you missed,' Colin was declaring. 'It was one of the best sights I've seen for weeks.'

Tariq was studying Erinna. 'No wonder you don't care for this character, if he's so rational, Erinna. We all know your dictum about not letting the head rule the heart.' He sighed gloomily. 'Mind you, it's like a foreign language to us poor scientists!'

'Rubbish! Scientists can be as sentimental as anyone else! It's just that John Bryce has the gall to pontificate on the inner meanings of poetry—even the Romantics, for God's sake!—when he's obviously impervious to the whole area of real emotions himself! I mean...'

'She's at it again.' The voice was cool, well-bred, supremely English. 'The lovely Erinna, stage centre, in the spotlight. What heavy theme are you so busy unfolding, Miss Casey?'

Everyone faced the intruder, then turned spontaneously to Erinna, as if to check her reaction to his arrival. She smiled and held her head high, but inside she was churning.

'Anthony! Where did you spring from?'

'Just got back from the pub with the rest of the Drama crowd. So come on, Erinna, aren't you going to tell me what's got you so rattled? Not that you're not gorgeous,' he added satirically, 'when you're roused.'

She gazed at him; she couldn't help herself. He was so blond and beautiful, so smooth and smart. Stylish, too, with trendy clothes and hair—image and attitude spot-on, exactly right for the streetwise fashions of the eighties. But beneath all that he was passionate, human—she sensed it, she could see it in the clear blue eyes and that sincere, heart-stopping smile. On stage a polished actor, but surely a breathing, *feeling* man, too.

She reflected that smile now, with her own most stunning one. In the presence of Anthony Travers she blossomed, externally at least. The painful thing was, secretly he made her feel like a gauche schoolgirl.

'Actually, we were discussing the great Dr Bryce,' she told him.

'Ah!' Anthony's eyes narrowed. 'That's interesting.'

'If you say so!' Erinna waved a dismissive hand.

'Erinna doesn't share the popular view of him,' Colin remarked.

'She reckons he's the worst thing since sliced bread,' Clare added.

'Erinna disapproves of sliced bread,' Lisa elaborated.

Mike was silent, but his eyes were still intent on Erinna.

Anthony laughed. 'Don't believe a word of it! You're his best student, everyone says so!'

'He only arrived here this year,' Erinna reminded them stiffly. 'We all got on perfectly well before he deigned to come among us.'

Anthony seemed keen to change the subject. He moved closer to Erinna, his gaze direct, his tone wonderfully warm and personal. 'I've come in search of you, Erinna. There's something I want to ask you.'

'Oh, yes?' This was a turn-up for the book! Anthony Travers, star of the Drama Society, every girl's fantasy but no one's property—come specifically looking for her? She stared at him suspiciously.

'Yes. It's about our next production. Dramsoc, you know.'

'You're doing *Much Ado About Nothing*, aren't you?'

'Right. I expect you've also heard I'm playing Benedick?'

'I'd heard.' Erinna's emerald eyes melted at the vision. She could imagine it only too clearly—Anthony as Benedick—one of the most dashing roles in the whole of Shakespeare! Perfect.

'God, I've just thought!' Clare erupted. 'Wasn't Becky Jones signed up to play the heroine? What's her name...you know...'

'Beatrice. Right.' Anthony nodded his fine fair head.

'So she was!' Erinna recalled Becky telling her about the successful audition for the part. She also recalled her own sensations when she'd heard who was playing Benedick. Pangs of pure, shameful jealousy. Then she remembered something more important. 'Becky? But she's...'

The others were not far behind her. 'She's ill! She won't be able to!'

'Right!' Anthony nodded again. They were getting the message. 'We're going to need a new Beatrice, and none of the other hopefuls were remotely possible. If you ask me,' he confided, dropping that well-modulated voice several tones, 'Becky only landed the part because she was going out with Julian.'

'Julian?' Tariq was lost among all these internal politics.

'Julian Tench, postgraduate, Drama Department,' Erinna informed him.

'He's the producer, isn't he?' Mike ventured.

'Right. Or was,' Anthony added, darkly.

'How do you mean, was?' Colin was barely keeping up with all this.

'Well, you know Becky's got this dreaded glandular fever?' Anthony stepped back, creating exactly the right space for maximum dramatic impact. 'Julian's gone down with it, too. She's been and gone and infected him.'

'No!' This was the best bit of scandal Clare had heard in months. 'I never knew it was *that* infectious!'

'You know what they call it.' Colin was grinning evilly. 'Kissing disease. It's not that infectious, unless you get...'

'Fairly intimate. Share a toothbrush, or—whatever.' Anthony grinned back. 'And as I say, they've been going out together. Now they've both been struck down by the nasty little virus, and we're left without a producer—or a leading lady.' He turned to Erinna again.

'I still don't see...' she began, but a spasm of excitement stirred in her stomach, fluttered her heart, shook her voice, just slightly.

'You're slow on the uptake, my lovely!' Anthony's smile was as charismatic as ever; then, suddenly, he was intense. 'Listen, Erinna, we all saw you in that charity revue thing last year, and we thought you were fantastic. You're a natural. I know you've never joined Dramsoc or thought of auditioning, but—well, we want to know if you'd consider taking on Beatrice. Stepping into the breach. We know you can do it.'

'Me?' Now Erinna's composure slipped completely, and her mouth fell open. The shock-wave rippled round the group, a mass of stares and exclamations. Anthony took no notice of any of them, only Erinna.

'Yes, you. You'd be fabulous, with your colouring and that glorious Irish lilt. And you know all about Shakespeare, the verse, obscure references and all that. I bet you've studied the play, haven't you?'

'Well, yes,' she admitted, almost on a whisper.

'Right. I knew you would have done. It shouldn't be hard for you to learn the part—there's the rest of this term, and a bit of next, before we perform it. We'd only just started rehearsals.'

'Well, I don't know...' But Erinna was radiant. To be invited—no, *implored*—to act a major role in one of her favourite plays. And opposite Anthony Travers, secret inhabitant of her private dreams...

But was she up to it? Fantasy would turn to nightmare if she let herself down in front of Anthony, when it mattered so much to him.

'I just don't know what to say,' she murmured.

Now the others leaped into life. 'Oh, go on, Erinna! Of course you should do it! He's right, you'd be great! You love acting, why not give it a whirl? Lucky you, chance would be a fine thing...'

Even the reticent Mike hardly concealed his delight. 'I think you ought to do it, Erinna. He's right, you were marvellous in the revue.'

Erinna glanced at each of them, then faced Anthony. She was never one to dither for very long.

'OK, I'll try! When's the next rehearsal?'

Anthony laughed aloud, caught her round the waist and swung her in the air. It was probably the most exhilarating moment of her life, but she smiled it off serenely. 'Hey, that's terrific, Erinna! Wait till I tell the rest of the cast! They'll be over the moon!' Setting her down, he leaned complacently against the bar. Erinna slumped on to a stool, getting her breath back. The others clustered about her, all jabbering at once.

'Since you're going to be involved, I feel better about asking you this other thing.'

There was an edge to Anthony's voice, a sharpness which alerted them. They all stared at him. 'What thing?' demanded Erinna.

'It's—it concerns Dr Bryce,' he said carefully.

'In what way?' Blast the man, he was cropping up everywhere today! What did he have to do with her hour of pride?

'I've just told you Julian's out of action. We need a producer.'

'Yes, but...' Erinna stood up. 'Oh, no! Not Bryce!' She backed physically away until she was up against the bar, as pale as she'd been flushed five minutes ago. 'Surely there must be someone...more...'

'There's no one better. There's no one at all, really. Anyway, why not?' Anthony launched into his suavest routine. 'I mean, leaving personal opinions aside, you must see he's the ideal man for the job? He's the big expert on the subject, and he used to direct lots of theatre when he was in Canada, or America, or Australia, or somewhere—I can't remember the details...' Anthony gestured vaguely, as if all these huge countries were equally alien and insignificant to this big fish in a small sea. 'And what a catch! To get his name on the posters!

With his reputation, we could fill every seat in the house three times over, no problem.'

'But Anthony...'

'Think of the play,' Anthony wheedled. 'You're part of a team now. You've got to consider the common cause, forget about your own prej——' He stopped himself just in time, and corrected 'prejudices' to 'preferences'. Anthony Travers was more than just a pretty face.

Erinna's conflict showed in her eyes, but she kept her dignity. 'Where do I come into all this? You don't need my permission, before...'

'Not your permission, no. Your help. If you asked him for us...'

'I couldn't do that, Anthony!'

'It's not on!' Lisa chimed in with her contribution, and not before time.

'He'll never do it,' Clare endorsed. 'Whoever asks him.'

'He rarely even has a drink with his postgraduates,' Colin said. 'Let alone participate in that sort of major event.'

'Doesn't sound too hopeful,' Tariq commented.

Once again, they were all looking at Erinna. Gaining strength from their support, she faced Anthony. 'Not a chance! Even if I could—even if I agreed to ask him, he'd never do it. He's away every Friday night and most Saturdays as it is. Sometimes he doesn't get back till Sunday evening. And when he's here, he makes a point of keeping...'

'I know all about that, but surely it's worth a try?' Anthony moved close to her again. The aura of him, the very smell of him, was so fresh and intoxicating. 'If we don't have a decent producer, there won't be a production. No one else is up to it, Julian said so himself.

If Dr Bryce could only be persuaded, I'm sure he'd enjoy it. After all, he is a leading light of the Arts Faculty. He owes the University a bit more than just his professional kudos, and a bare minimum of teaching. And you're his prize Finalist, right?'

'I wouldn't put it as strongly as that.' She was agonisingly torn between tension and exultation.

'You are, Erinna! You know you are!' The refrain came in like a Greek chorus. Whose side were they on, anyway?

'Right. So, added to that, you're a main part in the play. If *you* ask him, how can he refuse?' Anthony was so smooth. He should be a diplomat, not an actor. Perhaps he would be. Perhaps it came to the same thing.

'He's got a point, Erinna.' Colin was nodding energetically.

'You were saying how arrogant he is,' Lisa put in.

'Maybe it's time he sang a bit louder for his supper,' Tariq suggested.

'If anyone could persuade him, you could,' Clare maintained.

'You might as well try, Erinna,' Mike said quietly. 'It can't hurt.'

Couldn't it hurt? She stared at them all, so eager and expectant. Then at Anthony, so soft and beseeching—and surely there was affection in those eyes too, like a wistful puppy avid for her next move? He was so desirable, and she could be sharing the limelight with him, exchanging badinage with him...that brilliant, sexy banter between Benedick and Beatrice, all that attraction disguised as hostility before they finally learn to look into their hearts and confess their true feelings...

The ultimate in romantic relationships, and she could be bringing it to life with Anthony Travers! Working with him, touching him; who knew what might grow from that?

But now, the snag. In return—a kind of bargain—he wanted her to apply pressure to the stony Bryce. To use her influence on him, if she had any—which she doubted. Why should she succeed where all others had failed? If she did succeed, the play would go ahead, but she'd be forced to endure Bryce's company and atmosphere even more than she did already; several sessions a week, perhaps. But if she refused—or failed in the attempt— the play might never even happen, and what an opportunity to throw away!

It was her toughest dilemma yet, and she'd known a few. The others had gone silent now, but every gaze was fixed on her. Anthony knew when a pause carried more effect than a speech.

At last, when she continued dumb, he spoke, more gently. 'Tell you what, Erinna. Think it over till tomorrow. We don't have to know now.'

'No!' His words, the restraint in his tone, broke her paralysis. 'I'll be seeing him in the morning. I'll try and do it then...speak to him then. I won't promise anything, but I'll—I'll try, and I'll let you know what happens, tomorrow evening, OK?'

There was a general sigh of relief. As for Anthony, his beam shone through her.

'You're an angel, Erinna! I could kiss you!'

Feel free! her heart sang. But her most level voice replied, 'One day I might just hold you to that, Anthony. Meanwhile, you can buy me a drink. I don't know about the rest of you, but I need one.'

CHAPTER TWO

THE English Department was housed near the top of the newest block, with wide views of the campus and out to the countryside and suburbs beyond. Most days, when John Bryce stood at his office window, he gazed out on shades and textures of green and brown, punctuated with the greys of old stone and modern concrete, and the mellow red of brick. This Monday morning, the landscape was still wrapped in its blanket of relentless white.

Looking down, he could see small, purposeful figures converging on the building, singly and in groups, heading for their ten o'clock classes. Mostly undergraduates; some staff. He recognised many of them: there was old Dawes, Historian and Dean of Arts, shambling along, and that was Patterson, Professor of Philology, and young Embury, keen junior lecturer in French, busy chatting up the nearest attractive young female as usual. This one sported luminous green anorak, tight black ski-pants, scarlet boots, and a multi-striped scarf which flowed behind her in the blustery wind. As John watched, a ray of wintry sun emerged through the clouds and touched her hair with a brilliant auburn glow.

It was Erinna, of course. On her way up here, to this study. Punctual for once, shabby briefcase tucked under one arm, bulging with folders full of competent notes and articulate essays. What was she expecting to discuss with him today? Wordsworth, wasn't it? Well, he had a few surprises for her; she needn't think she was the only one who could be unpredictable.

John was acutely aware of the general opinion of him—unbending, unapproachable—and he positively encouraged it, among students and colleagues alike. Keeping them at bay suited him, leaving him free to pursue his private concerns when he wasn't fulfilling his obligations here at the University. But there were times when even he felt driven by instinct, rather than logic. He hadn't quite worked out why, but this seemed to be one of them.

Now he walked quickly to his desk and sat down behind an untidy fortress of books and papers, dark head bent in concentration, pen in hand. When it came to confronting Erinna Casey, he must be fully prepared. She was his brightest Finalist, the one with the highest hopes of an excellent degree. She was also his most challenging, and not just intellectually.

John might be superficially reserved, but he was not self-deluded. He hadn't just fallen off the tree, and he knew his reactions to this girl were complex. Something about her—this mercurial quality, this sharp vitality— quickened his blood as well as his temper. His mental responses to her fairly outrageous notions were alarmingly violent, and he was not such a fool as to deny that they sprang from responses at a deeper level. Anger and attraction—classic first cousins.

At least he had learned to recognise the danger, even if he had scarcely begun to process it. Years of experience had made him an expert, not just in the public arena of Shakespeare and Marlowe, Byron and Shelley, but also in the private matter of dealing with precisely this kind of threat. Keeping those responses safely submerged until they receded. Up to now, they had always receded, and he was confident they would this time. After all, the fair Ms Casey only had a few months of tutorials before her Finals; unless she decided to stay on for a

postgraduate degree, in which case his iron self-control
might be stretched to the limit and he would certainly
have to have her transferred to...

She had a firm, extrovert knock. He knew it
immediately.

'Come!'

She was not one of those who peered round the door,
hesitated, then tiptoed gingerly in as if he was likely to
bite their heads off—literally, you might think, seeing
some of their apprehensive faces. No, she always
marched in, smiled broadly, closed the door behind her
with one foot, and made for her favourite chair.

'Good morning, Erinna.'

'Good morning, Dr Bryce. I hope you've recovered
from yesterday?'

'Yesterday?' What the hell was the woman on about
now?

'Your...our slight mishap.'

'Oh, that!' He smiled, leaning back in his chair,
stretching his long, denim-clad legs under the desk. 'I'd
forgotten all about it!'

She gazed at him, green eyes direct as ever. 'That's
all right, then.' She knew, and so did he, that it was far
from true. The escapade might have slipped his conscious mind, but underneath he was still smarting.

'No damage done, except to my dignity.'

Still that rare, steady smile, lucid grey eyes returning
her inspection. She seemed disappointed at this serene
restraint. So, she'd expected him to be reproachful, or
insulted, had she? She'd have to adjust her ideas, then.
Tactics, thought John; this was only the beginning. I
don't have to conform to your preconceptions, my lady!

'I'm sorry it happened. It was an accident, as I said.'

John was unconvinced, but he merely nodded. 'Yes,
you said, and I forgave you. My tracksuits dried on the

radiator, no problem. I had a drop of Scotch—without the milk.' He grimaced.

Erinna was settling herself opposite him, and scrabbling in her bag for the relevant file. 'I'm relieved to hear it,' she said sweetly.

'Now...' He leaned on the desk, pushing a few books and papers out of the way. 'Before you get too organised, Erinna, I have a proposition for you.'

She paused in mid-scrabble. 'What sort of proposition?'

'No need to look so paranoid. Nothing immoral.'

'Perish the thought, Dr Bryce!' Now it was her turn to switch on that incandescent smile, while he felt himself go woodenly solemn.

'I gather poor Becky is well and truly out of action?'

'That's right. She might have to go home. She certainly won't be coming to tutorials for a few weeks, but not to worry, I've made some notes on "Intimations of Immortality" and we can still...'

'Steady on!' He held up a hand, as that lilting voice picked up speed. 'That's the point. Since it appears to be just you and me, I thought we might cut the Wordsworth and proceed to something more...'

'*Cut* the Wordsworth? But it's on my special paper! Just because we haven't got Becky, or her essay, surely it doesn't mean we can't...'

'No call to get so steamed up, Erinna,' he soothed. 'We haven't even started on anything yet. Keep your enviable energy for a more constructive target.'

She surveyed him with mingled hostility and disdain, but he was used to handling that. 'So, what did you have in mind, Dr Bryce?'

'This.' He pulled a slim volume from the chaos in front of him, and held it up for her to see.

'*The Collected Works of W.B. Yeats*. Yeats?' She frowned, wrinkling her nose as well as her brow. 'Why?'

'Why not? This is a general poetry paper. Good old Wordsworth will keep until Becky is with us again. And anyway, I thought you might have a particular interest in Yeats.'

'But we're only supposed to have reached the nineteenth century! And why should I have a particular interest in Yeats?'

'Are you being deliberately obtuse, Erinna? No reason why you *should*; I just thought you probably *would*.'

'Because of being Irish, you mean?'

'Something like that,' he agreed drily.

There was a short pause, then she tossed her head and admitted, 'Well, as it happens, you're right. I think Yeats is great.'

'There you are, then.' He slid the book across to her, and rummaged among the mess. 'I'm sure I had another copy here. That's the library one, and I got my own out specially...'

'But won't it matter if we don't do the listed tutorial topic?'

'Erinna.' He found the book and held it between his palms as he studied her. 'It's not like you to be so rule-bound! I expected more spirit of adventure from you, of all people. What's with all this anxiety about sticking rigidly to a syllabus?'

'It's a bit sudden, that's all. I'm not prepared, and I haven't read Yeats for a while, or made any notes, or...'

The more edgy she grew, the more he became smooth and fluent. 'No problem. I won't expect a detailed familiarity with the text. This is what they pay me for,' he reminded her sardonically. 'Imparting gems of information to the likes of you. At the very least, sharing my treasure-house of knowledge.'

'I do realise that, Dr Bryce.' She was looking down at the book in her hands. When she looked up again, she was smiling. 'Fair enough. There's no reason on earth why Yeats shouldn't crop up on our special paper, after all, now is there?'

John shook his head and tutted. 'You know I'm not in a position to answer that one, Erinna. Let's just say, it can't do any harm to consider him. And you wouldn't want to neglect your most famous literary compatriot, would you?'

'Oh, I don't think I'd regard Yeats as our most celebrated writer. What about Joyce, or Swift, or...'

'Let's not get bogged down in pointless or invidious comparisons.' John was opening his copy of the poems. 'Now, what I thought...'

'Bogged down! Was that meant to be funny?'

'What?' He glanced up. 'Oh, I see, bogged... bogs...Irish. No, it wasn't, it was totally unintentional.' He grinned, a bit stiffly. 'You're so sharp, you'll cut yourself.'

'Huh!' But she grinned back, eager now, putting him in mind of a fine thoroughbred chestnut mare, pawing the ground before a race.

He leaned back again, only half aware of lengthening the space between them, reinforcing the solid barrier of his desk. 'So, could we turn our attention to William B, 1865 to 1939? For instance...' John's eyes narrowed, briefly and imperceptibly, as he focused his aims. He might call this a plan of action. He'd been waiting to broach this topic with Erinna, challenge her on it, shake her out of that naïve set of convictions which sat so uncomfortably with that acute brain. Adolescent, almost, among the notable maturity she displayed otherwise.

'For instance?' she nudged, as he appeared lost in thought.

He shook himself. He intended to take the reins, not drift off like some absent-minded professor! That wasn't his style at all.

'For instance, we've been studying Coleridge and Shelley recently. Now, doesn't Yeats make a stark contrast with them?'

'How do you mean?' She eyed him suspiciously. The challenge must be creeping into his tone, because he was choosing his words with extreme care, keeping them bland and technical.

'Self-evident, surely?' He adopted his most breezy manner. 'They're the great Romantics, as opposed to Yeats.'

'You mean to say you don't consider Yeats to be a romantic?' Erinna was aghast, as he had calculated.

'Not entirely. Mystic, even visionary, yes. But wouldn't you say he was a poet of ideas, in the final analysis?'

'How can you talk such rubbish? Everyone knows Yeats was one of the greatest expressors of feelings!'

'Then everyone must have failed to tell me,' John observed.

Erinna might be volatile, but she was always sensitive. 'I'm sorry, I didn't mean to be rude, only I thought...'

'Don't be silly.' Still leaning back, John tapped the end of his pen on the desk. 'It's not rude to disagree with me. That's what I'm here for—up to a point. I say Yeats was not a true romantic, you say he was. So, state your case.'

Erinna was searching frantically through the pages. Her blood was already up, John could tell from her expression and colour. He watched dispassionately, fingertips pressed together, dark head to one side.

'Well, there are obvious examples, like my favourite, this one. "He Wishes for the Cloths of Heaven".'

John nodded sagely, as if he had known she would cite this example. '"But I, being poor, have only my dreams; I have spread my dreams under your feet...",' he drawled, as if quoting a laundry list.

'Exactly!' Erinna was arrested in the act of flicking through the book. There was something not right about the way he said those lovely lines—soft and low, but with a harsh undertone which made a mockery of the beautiful sentiments. 'What could be more romantic than that?' She found another poem and scanned the page for a few seconds. 'What about this wonderful bit about "the silver apples of the moon, the golden apples of the sun"?'

John's gaze was stern now on her face. 'In my opinion, there's a clear strand of irony in much of Yeats' so-called expressive verse, even these particularly lyrical passages. We must beware of taking literature—not to mention life—at face value, Erinna. These words and phrases were chosen by a master for maximum effect of sound and sentiment, but when we apply reason, rather than emotion, to our analysis of them, we often find cynicism and disillusion. We should be on our guard against confusing style with meaning.'

Having delivered this homily, he folded his arms and stared at her harder than ever. She was fidgeting and frowning—rising superbly to his bait. Easier than taking sweets from an infant! Easier than hurling a snowball at an unsuspecting jogger.

'But surely,' Erinna protested, 'if it *sounds* romantic—if it *feels* romantic—then it is?'

One of the most effective Bryce teaching techniques was to play devil's advocate, and this was his best opportunity yet. In a way, he and Erinna were both right, but he wasn't explaining that to her in words of one syllable. Life wasn't so simple or clear-cut, but she'd have to work it out for herself—the hard way. He was doing this for her own sake, from purely academic motives, naturally.

'Perhaps,' he suggested now, 'it's time we defined what we mean by that overworked concept, romantic?'

'That's easy!' She drew a deep breath. 'It's a sort of imaginative sympathy...sensitivity to nature and human feelings...a search for perfection in experience and emotion...awareness of the senses...'

John chuckled, but he was impressed. 'Sounds pretty comprehensive. You've evidently given the question some thought. And at least you refrained from saying "pertaining to true love": cue swooping violins and rosy sunset.'

'For God's sake, Dr Bryce! Give me credit for some intelligence! I do happen to know we're not talking about slushy stories, or films with happy-ever-after endings...'

'But true love does come into it somewhere?' he pressed.

'It certainly does! How could it fail to, if we're talking about human feelings, and experience?'

He had really reached the spot now, touched that raw nerve, but so far she was in control of her temper, poised between dignity and defiance. It was a delicate business, seeing how far he could push her. John had to admit to himself that he was relishing it.

'Yet you still maintain Yeats was a romantic?'

'He *was*!' She found another poem, and jabbed a finger at it. 'I mean, we all know this one: "When you are old and grey and full of sleep..."'

John chimed in again, in that automatic, semi-chanting tone—as if he resented doing it, but could barely help himself. '"Murmur, a little sadly, how Love fled,

And paced upon the mountain overhead, And hid his face amid a crowd of stars".'

'There you are!' Erinna was triumphant. 'Nothing, but nothing, could be more profoundly romantic than that!'

'Hmmm.' She was keeping her wits, making out a fair case, but John had not increased the pressure yet. 'Sentimental, really. What's more, he's hardly describing true and endless love. Isn't he saying you can't trust love, or youth, or anything beautiful and good, to last? That strikes me as entirely realistic, not to say pessimistic.'

'But you can be romantic and realistic at the same time!' Erinna's voice was as steady as ever, but the words fair machine-gunned at him. He had a job not to flinch physically from the attack. 'What about Keats, in "Ode to a Nightingale"? We were only saying, a few weeks ago, about that bit, you know: "Youth grows pale, and spectre-thin, and dies..." So, where do we draw the line? I still say this *is* a romantic poem, and Yeats *is* a romantic poet; and not just his language, his meaning as well.'

She was gaining ground. It was time John backed up his own argument with examples, and that wasn't going to be quite so easy. 'OK, how about this for realism— "Romantic Ireland's dead and gone, it's with O'Leary in the grave"?'

'But that's political, not personal. That's different.'

'Yeats wouldn't have drawn that distinction, any more than Wordsworth would. They were both fervent revolutionaries, until...'

'And revolutionaries are notoriously romantic!' Erinna clearly considered he had scored an own-goal. She was on the edge of her chair, flushed with a Celtic fervour no less vivid than Yeats'.

John scrutinised her. She was showing admirable staying power. Few students had ever stood up to him with such vehemence or integrity. He knew just how intimidating they found him. If they hadn't, he'd have been alarmed to find his effect slipping.

It was time to tighten the screw, to change to another tack, even more deadly but just as subtle.

'Then of course,' he observed, 'there are Yeats' theories about women in general. Not exactly liberal, in your estimation, I should imagine?'

'How do you mean?' Erinna was guarded.

'He dismissed them as fickle; sensual, but shallow.' John turned a few pages, and suddenly quoted, still in that odd deadpan voice, '"Never give all the heart, for love will hardly seem worth thinking of to passionate women..."'

'"If it seem certain",' Erinna chimed in, '"and they never dream that it fades out from kiss to kiss."' She had read the lines, reflected on them, absorbed them so often, they were like a private anthem to her. Yeats had captured her own feelings and philosophy precisely. '"For everything that's lovely",' she completed it, her voice lyrical, her eyes bright, '"is but a brief, dreamy, kind delight."'

If John had expected her to find these comments offensively sexist, he was disappointed. On the contrary, she seemed spellbound. Illogical, unpredictable to the last! Dropping his gaze to the page, he echoed those final words, as if unable to prevent them. '"A brief, dreamy, kind delight."' Then he cleared his throat. 'So, you don't take issue with Yeats' assessment of the female psyche?'

Erinna was smiling. 'I'd say he understood us pretty well—some of us, at least. Anyway, Dr Bryce, isn't this a traditional aspect of romance? Dating back to its medieval roots? Treating the whole female sex as special, separate, a bit mysterious, elusive?'

But John had his ace of trumps to play yet. 'It's not quite as simple as that. Not so ethereal—more earthy. He denies women any intellect. In fact, you might say he was the arch-male-chauvinist, under all the spurious chivalry.'

Erinna was ready for that one. 'That figures. It goes with the whole business of putting women on a pedestal, not seeing them as real. It still doesn't prove he wasn't a romantic.' She was looking through the book again as she spoke, and found what she wanted. 'You mean all this..."Must no beautiful woman be learned, like a man?"'

'Exactly. He says reading and thinking can't be any good to women, because—how does it go?—"what mere book can grant a knowledge...appropriate to that beating breast, that vigorous thigh, that dreaming eye?"'

John was outwardly calmer than ever, but he disguised a tension, a frisson, at declaiming those evocative phrases aloud to Erinna Casey, who might be the embodiment of them.

'And you don't call *that* romantic, either?' she was demanding now.

'Not really. I find it realistic. That's what I've been saying. Look between the lyrical lines, and Yeats was essentially a humanist. Far too sensible a view of the world to be dismissed as romanticism...'

At last Erinna's temperature was visibly rising again, and John grew all the cooler. 'I suppose you agree with all that *sensible* stuff? About females being all soft—emotionally strong but intellectually weak? You would, of course—you, of all men! It gives you the excuse to just go on being hard and rational, leave all the true work to us!'

John shrugged complacently. 'What difference does it make, what I believe? We're delving into W.B. Yeats, not me!'

Now Erinna's tone was rising, along with her colour—high tide, washing over those striking cheekbones. It had taken him far longer than he had anticipated to crack that clever, stubborn front—especially in view of the fact that he had sprung this whole subject on her without warning. If this had been a battle, it was certainly ending in nothing more ignominious than a draw.

Yes, he would give this session a high grade in her continuous assessment scale. Probably an alpha-minus, or at the very least a beta-plus-plus. Never mind his personal position, she deserved it...

But suddenly she was on her feet, and glaring. His last words had toppled her over an edge, and now she clutched the side of his desk, white at the knuckles, eyes flashing an unbridled defiance.

'That's it, isn't it, Dr Bryce? We've hit the nail there, haven't we? None of this means a thing to you, does it? Where are you—the real you, the person, the man? It's been just so many empty words...concepts... technicalities! Verse form, imagery, that's the level you operate on. Metaphor and simile, rhyme and rhythm, romantic and realistic...it's all the same to you! Jargon, meaningless jargon. I don't care how famous you are, how erudite—I don't know how you have the *nerve* to teach poetry at all! I don't know how you *dare* to set yourself up as some kind of expert—guru—pundit, reeling off all this—this *dross* about emotional expression, when you quite obviously wouldn't recognise a real feeling if it rose up and hit you in the face!'

She subsided, but only to draw breath. The outburst was so abrupt and so intense, even for Erinna, that John

could only stare. Then he spoke, and his tone was carefully flat and flippant.

'It's funny you should say that, Erinna. Only yesterday, one did rise up and hit me in the face, and bloody
cold it was, too!'

For a few seconds she groped for a retort, and he had
never seen her so enraged. It was such a contrast, after
all the cerebral, level argument. And now this on-
slaught, this eruption...

'That just about says it all—just about sums you up,
Dr Bryce! Only you could compare a snowball with a
feeling! Oh, I know you were being funny, making a
joke out of it, but actually you were nearer the mark
than you think. That's probably as close to a true
emotion as you're ever likely to get. Icy, formless, and
melting away before it's ever really existed!'

She was so agitated, John had risen to his feet too,
and was leaning over his desk. 'Erinna, listen, I was
only...'

'I don't care what you were doing! I don't want to
know, and I don't want any more to do with your so-
called tutorials, or your lectures or your seminars, or
anything to do with you! You don't know what you're
on about! People like you should be banned from having
any connection with poetry! Pontificating, all those
words of wisdom—as if a man like you could *really*
understand what poets are trying to say! You're all head,
John Bryce! Look at the way you've just pushed me into
a corner with all that stuff about Yeats—or tried to,'
she added, with a touch of justifiable pride.

'No, Erinna, you've got to let me explain.' John was
determined to squeeze a few words in edgeways, but
Erinna wasn't having any.

'Oh, it was no more than a formal debate to you, I
see that—a mental exercise, a test to keep the grey cells

in trim, yours and mine! Keep us both on our intellectual toes! Never mind the *real* content of what we were discussing, *real* warmth, desire, agony, hope, fear— all pouring out of those wonderful lines! You've got it pared down to a soulless, mathematical equation, haven't you? Romantic and realistic. Now I suppose you want to send me away with an essay to write on that neat little theme. Well, you can whistle for your essay, Dr Bryce, because I'm not going to! Nor am I coming back here. You can keep your facts and figures for those who are idiot enough to appreciate them. I prefer to deal in sentiments and sensations. I chose to study literature, not algebra!'

Surely she must be running out of steam now? John was half-way round his desk, one arm outstretched, concerned enough to leave his haven and approach her. 'Listen to me, Erinna Casey. You're getting it all...'

But she had been retreating during that last declamation, grabbing her briefcase, and now she was near the door. Before he could reach her, she had opened it and fled, slamming it behind her. Even as he crossed the room, he could hear her fast light step, resounding through the hollow spaces of the bare building.

'*Erinna!*' Not caring who heard him, John strode along the corridor. Had she hurtled downstairs, or might she still be summoning the lift? No, it must have been conveniently there, all ready for her to charge into; the lift dial told him it was already at the third floor, and descending. Without a doubt, containing a seething Erinna.

Could anyone or anything ever contain such force of character? She was fascinating, all right—difficult, prickly, but so alive...

And now, what was he going to do? Return to his office, wait for the next lot to arrive—it was ten-forty,

she had stormed out twenty minutes early—or take decisive action, as impulse was urging him to?

He hesitated, but only for a split second. Then he was
off down the stairs, all nine flights of them. When he
wanted to, John Bryce could really move, and he wanted
to now. It was out of the question to leave this situation
unresolved. OK, he confessed it to himself: his own
strategy, his own sense of pique, had backfired on him.
But she was his best student, and he couldn't risk her
results or the rapport they had built up—couldn't bear
the weight of responsibility for this. No, he would find
her and have it out with her, tidy things up, smooth things
over. He was good at that: tact, discretion...these hitches
can always be sorted out with a judicious helping of sweet
reason.

Fifth floor...fourth...third. His step was fast and
regular on the concrete stairs, pounding out a beat, his
own momentum driving him on. In his head, those last
lines of his favourite Yeats poem formed themselves and
repeated themselves, echoing over and over as he ran.
His favourite—and Erinna's.

> 'But I, being poor, have only my dreams;
> I have spread my dreams under your feet;
> Tread softly because you tread on my dreams.'

CHAPTER THREE

THE lift was a welcome friend, bearing Erinna down-wards, away from the wretched Bryce. She leaned in a corner, eyes closed, concentrating on long, slow breaths. Then she turned and pressed her overheated face against the cold, metal wall: first her burning brow, then one flushed cheek, then the other.

Drat the man, how had he achieved it? She'd pre-sented herself this morning, serenely alert for a stimu-lating but unthreatening session of Wordsworth and his theories on the immortality of the soul. So how was it that John Bryce had twisted everything up? Confused her thoughts, aggravated her feelings, tensed her nerves—and clearly stayed so infuriatingly cool in the process.

More to the point, why? Why produce this peculiar Yeats number today, out of the blue, when he'd always kept strictly to the syllabus before? Then why use it as a trigger for releasing this clash between them? As if he'd been waiting for the right opportunity to get at her—attack her on this level? He knew her well enough by now to understand how deep the whole subject went. These last forty minutes had been a lot more than a simple literary conflict. They'd both known about the bone of contention that simmered not far below the surface, but it was Bryce who had chosen to air it. He had questioned her integrity, even mocked her inmost beliefs, her raw self—and he'd done it with careful cal-culation, she could see that already, despite her agitation.

Malice aforethought, that was the expression. It was despicable, nothing short of cruel, downright unnecessary! And if it had anything to do with their little accident—no, incident—yesterday, it was positively juvenile. At least she'd kept her pride, making her point before making her dramatic exit! She trusted he'd take her insults to heart, always assuming he *had* a heart beating under that robotic exterior. Presumably even the blood of the august Bryce needed pumping round that well-tuned frame by some means other than sheer brainpower?

Too bad if this had jeopardised her chances of a First. It had been worth it to see his face when she let rip with those pent-up home truths. Some areas of life were more significant than academic or worldly success. What could the stony Bryce know of relationships and commitments, passion, personal honour, and . . .

Commitments! The lift bumped to a halt at the ground floor, just as an uncomfortable recollection bumped Erinna's mind. In the turmoil, she had completely forgotten her promise to Anthony. Today of all days, it had been vital to keep John Bryce as sweet as possible, so that she could convey that urgent request, not just on Anthony's behalf, but the whole Dramsoc. That major responsibility, all those people depending on her, and she'd been and gone and screwed it up by screaming at the great man like a fishwife, instead of lulling him into an amenable mood!

'Oh, Anthony!' Erinna lamented, as the lift doors opened. 'How could I be so stupid? So selfish?'

The lobby stretched ahead to the full-length glass at the entrance, and then all that arctic air and crisp snow. Erinna sighed, reaching to wrap her padded anorak snugly round her and zip it up against the sharp wind.

What anorak? In the stress of the moment she had automatically seized her bag and briefcase, but her coat was still draped across the chair she'd been sitting on.

Pathetic idiot! She'd stormed out of a heatwave and into an ice age, protected only by a primrose sweatshirt. Cosy enough in these central-heated conditions, but a recipe for disaster if she planned to walk all the way back to her block with nothing over it. Five minutes, and she'd be shivering. Ten, and she'd be numb. Not to mention the next time she had to go out...

No, it wouldn't do; and anyway, there was this other matter to sort out. Erinna's temper might flare in an instant, but the flames tended to bank down almost as fast. Even if the embers went on glowing, she usually had enough strength and self-respect to offer the olive branch first, and soon, rather than letting resentments fester. This time was going to be tough, but crucial because she hadn't only got herself to consider. She had Anthony, and all the cast of the play.

The play! Such a stirring prospect! But without a producer, as Anthony had wisely pointed out, there could be no production. And without a production she'd miss this magic chance to act opposite Anthony.

Right, that clinched it. Before she could chicken out, she pressed the button for the ninth floor. The doors slid together, the lift jerked into action, carrying her upwards as inexorably as it had carried her down.

Meanwhile, John Bryce leaped the last four stairs and ran across the lobby and out into the wintry morning. That Siberian wind lifted his thick dark hair and sliced through his jeans and check shirt, but unlike Erinna he neither noticed nor cared. Catching up with the woman, that was top priority. But where the hell *was* she? She must have moved amazingly fast, but in which direction? He gazed round, shading his eyes against the pale glare of sun on snow. A few people wandered, strolled or marched about, but none of them was Erinna Casey.

Damn and blast! He'd have to take a chance, follow a hunch, and head for the Union. Knowing Erinna, she'd probably drop into the cafeteria for a soothing coffee, and the even more soothing excuse to unburden herself on the topic of the ghastly Dr Bryce, if she happened to meet a friend. It was worth a try. Hunching his shoulders, he set off at a brisk trot for the Union building, five minutes away.

He had hardly gone three paces before an instinct caused him to stop dead. There were eyes fixed on him, he could swear it. Someone was staring at him; he could feel their whole attention drilling into his back. It prickled, like a physical touch.

He swung round. Nobody there, of course. He cursed himself for a fool and prepared to run on; every second counted, and here he was, wasting them! On a whim, he turned his gaze upwards, sweeping the blank windows of the block he had just left. At least, most of them were blank, but wasn't that a figure, standing behind that one—up there at the top—which must be very near his own room? There was something about it; it was too far away for John to see clearly, but he was irrationally certain it was focused on him, sending out the beam of a summons direct to him.

He frowned and muttered at his own flights of fancy, and was about to take off in the opposite direction when the figure moved, catching a shaft of sunlight. The red of its hair and the yellow of its sweater were perfectly clear to John. In the same moment, its features appeared, minutely detailed in his mind's eye.

It *was* his room, and that person at his window was Erinna Casey! Glaring down at him like a spectre of their recent altercation, haunting the battleground. Four minutes ago he'd been up there and she'd been hurtling down here. So what was going on? What sort of surreal, topsy-turvy business was this? She was an unfathomable creature, he didn't deny it; he wouldn't put it past her to be wired into some mysterious current with power to reverse the film—cast leprechaun spells over his actions!

A particularly vicious gust assaulted him, as if to haul him back to logical reality. 'O! that this too too solid flesh...' John tore his gaze from the vision at the window and re-entered the building.

Erinna was waiting for him, sedate in the same chair, hands folded in her lap as if she'd never moved. John closed the door and leaned on it, scrutinising that demure back view until she swivelled round to confront him.

It was Erinna who broke the silence, all gentle solicitude. 'I hope you came up in the lift, Dr Bryce?'

'I did, as a matter of fact. I decided it was quite important not to be devoid of breath, on top of everything else.'

'I came back,' she explained.

'So it would seem.'

'I left my coat.' The more sweet and low her voice, the more heavily he frowned. 'Were you coming after me, Dr Bryce?'

'Evidently. You see, I wanted...'

'No,' she interrupted, with sudden vehemence. '*I* want to apologise. It was my fault, I shouldn't get so touchy, and I shouldn't mix my—my private preoccupations with work, and I shouldn't have said the things I did. I must try not to get so steamed up. I'm sorry.'

She wasn't taking a word of it back, but that didn't make the apology any less sincere or abject. She recited it without faltering, which was hardly surprising considering she'd been rehearsing it these last five minutes. Now she watched him, anxious for his reaction.

His frown had evaporated; that was something. But he remained very tense. 'I wasn't about to offer regrets or excuses, Erinna, but I do want to explain what I was getting at. That's why I came after you, and that's why I'm glad you came back. I didn't feel we could or should leave things like that between us. There's more than enough futile aggro around without us adding to it. Life's too short.' To her relieved astonishment, a grin actually broke through the stern veneer. 'And the academic year's even shorter. You and I can't afford to squander our precious tutorial time in pointless wrangles, eh?'

'Just what I was thinking.' Erinna smiled back. Thank God! This might not turn out as tricky as she'd feared. One notable plus in dealing with the super-rational Bryce—at least he could take such dramas in his stride, without blowing a fuse. And talking of dramas...

Now he was crossing the room; Erinna turned her chair so that she still faced him. This time he leaned on the edge of his desk, rather than taking refuge behind it.

'Erinna,' he demanded abruptly, 'what were you actually doing at the window?'

'What do you mean, doing?' She felt a wave of paranoia. Did his unruffled mask conceal an inner fury, biding its time?

'I mean just what I say. Did you simply hope I'd happen to look up and see you, or what?' His interest seemed almost scientific.

'When I got back here and found you gone, I realised what must have happened, so I went to the window. When I saw you down there, I tried to open it, but——'

'You can't,' he cut in. 'They're permanently sealed up. All very well in this weather, but I loathe not breathing real air in the summer.'

He was bland, as if they'd spent the whole time on such trivial conversation; but two could play at that game.

'Oh, I agree!' Erinna nodded vigorously. 'Anyway, so then I banged on the glass. I thought it must be too high up for you to hear, but obviously you did, so that was all right.'

John studied her, then shrugged. Of course he hadn't heard her knocking. It was scarcely likely, with a force eight gale blowing, and from nine storeys up, on a double-glazed, sealed unit. But if she preferred to believe he had, that suited him fine.

'So, here we are again! With just ten minutes left to—what shall we say, tidy things up? OK, Erinna, I accept your apology, for the second time in as many days. Once again, no bones broken. Mind you, I'm not at all sure which I find the most daunting: having lumps of snow hurled at me, or personal abuse.'

She returned a quick, guarded grin, but her green eyes were steady, even stubborn, on his. 'Thank you, Dr Bryce. And you still insist that Yeats wasn't a romantic? Not even inclined that way?'

It was John's turn to be gracious. 'No, I don't insist that at all. Yeats was no less susceptible to the tug-of-war between head and heart than the rest of us.'

Including you? Surely not! But Erinna nodded gravely, adopting her enthralled-pupil expression as she allowed him to embark on his explanation, or justification, or elaboration, or whatever he was intent on giving. She had to get him into a receptive frame of mind, and she had only a few minutes left to do it.

'I'm sure you'll realise when you think about it,' he was continuing, 'with the benefit of hindsight and all that, Erinna, that I was alienating you deliberately. Polarising our two positions, you might say.'

Hiding a twinge of irritation, she suggested, 'So that I would see your point for myself?'

'Exactly. No poet—no person,' he corrected, 'is irrevocably fixed at either of those two extremes. We all drift up and down a scale between them, don't we? We're all a mass of paradoxes and contradictions. Yeats was no exception. Nor are you.' He hesitated. 'Nor am I.'

Erinna risked a cautious question, keeping tight reins on herself. 'But why Yeats? I mean, any of the poets we've been studying would have done to make that point, wouldn't they? Keats, who was a doctor as well as a dreamer, or...'

John hooked his thumbs into his belt. 'I suppose they would. I chose Yeats because he seemed a specially suitable vehicle, being Irish and all, as well as representing that particular dichotomy rather...'

'Yes, I do see.' Erinna must bring this literary discussion to a close, so that she could introduce other, more pressing matters. 'Next time I'll try and keep my reactions rational,' she promised.

'Next time?' His eyes narrowed.

'Oh, you have every right to be sceptical, Dr Bryce, but I really...'

'No, I didn't mean that. I meant, you plan to come again, then?'

'Why on earth not?' She was genuinely surprised.

'I've accepted your apology, but you haven't mentioned whether you've forgiven *me*.'

'Oh!' This was unexpected, but she dealt with it calmly. 'There's nothing to forgive. I'm sure I asked for all I got. Call it quits, shall we, Dr Bryce?'

He inclined his head. 'Quits.' Then he moved away, towards the bulging bookcase near his desk. 'So, perhaps next time we might consider a more contemporary Irish poet. There's a rich vein, and it could be useful to draw a few comparisons...' His index finger trailed the titles on some shiny paperbacks. 'What about Seamus Heaney? Or this recent series of Derry Jaffares?'

Erinna's eyes and mind were ahead of him, further along the same shelf. 'Hey, you've got the new collection by Devin O'Connor! I've got all his stuff, he's fantastic!' Her tone had come alive, her face alight. 'Now, if you're looking for a poet of *feelings*, a true spokesman for humanity in all its joys and sufferings— how did that old line go? "What oft was thought but ne'er so well expressed"... Devin O'Connor's got to be your man!'

John was still engrossed in the contents of his shelves. 'So, you give O'Connor the Casey seal of approval, eh? Hmmm, well, later on we might look at one or two of his, but what I had in mind was really someone more... less...'

'More what? Less what?' He was so abstracted, Erinna's temper began to rise again. 'No one could repay analysis better than O'Connor! No poet of any age or any nationality!'

'That's a bit excessive isn't it?' Now John did turn to face her. 'I mean, he may be competent enough, but not one of the greats, surely?'

'Well, you would think that, with your insistence on balance between the pragmatic and the romantic!' Erinna was off the deep end again, blazing up the instant the spark had been struck. 'But you can't have studied him very hard, or you'd know he really does achieve that essential combination. He's so warm and lyrical, but at the same time he's a brilliant craftsman, always in control of his medium. He has this facility with words, so that we know just what he means, because we've felt exactly the same. We've been there ourselves, even if we hardly realised we had. You know what I mean, Dr Bryce? Isn't that what poetry ought to be all about?'

She managed to contain the outburst, ending on a meeker note than she had begun, just in time. John waited for the torrent of enthusiasm to abate, impassive as ever.

'Some might say so, Erinna. I'm sorry, but I can't get into all this again now.' He glanced at his watch. 'A trio of keen second-years is due any minute, and I'm committed to regaling them on the themes and sources of *Love's Labours Lost*.'

'Oh, no! Not yet!' References to Shakespeare, and commitment, dragged Erinna down to earth with a crash.

'Not yet? Good grief, haven't you had enough of me for one day?'

'No, it's not that. I haven't...I mean, I have, but...oh, damn!' Thoroughly flustered, Erinna scrambled to her feet and retired behind her chair, clutching it for moral support. John leaned on his desk, watching her with a clear, objective curiosity.

'If you have something else to say, Erinna, you'll have to say it now.'

'Yes, I have.' She squared up to him, reminding herself how much was at stake. 'But it's not about our work, or at least not directly. It's a great favour I want to ask you, on behalf of some friends of mine. Well, on my own behalf too, but...' After all the build-up, she was making a proper hash of this. What price all her fluency now? Typical of it, to desert her at the moment of crisis.

John was still staring at her—rather coldly, she thought. 'All this sounds highly intriguing,' he commented.

'The thing is, it's like this...did you know the Drama Society are putting on *Much Ado About Nothing* this year?'

'I believe I had heard, yes. Why?'

'Well, Julian Tench, who is supposed to be directing it, has had to drop out. He's Becky's boyfriend.'

'I dare say I'll make a connection any second now.'

Erinna fought to retain a shred of dignity. 'Becky's got glandular fever, right?'

'Right.'

'And so has Julian!' she declared, as if that explained everything.

'Ahh!' John nodded earnestly. '*Now* I'm with you. There was a connection, but it was between Julian and Becky. How unfortunate for them both,' he added. 'I hope you'll send them my very best wishes for a speedy recovery.'

It was really impossible to tell whether he was satirical, or polite, or plain bored. Erinna braced herself and came to the point.

'Look, Dr Bryce, we desperately need a good producer, or director, or whatever you call it, and I promised I'd—well, I'd ask you!'

There, it was out at last! She'd done her best, and now it was over to him. He had picked up a book from his desk and was riffling through the pages as if it was the most riveting object in the world. Erinna held her peace for what felt like several minutes; then she could bear the suspense no longer.

'Dr Bryce?'

He looked up. 'Am I getting this right? They—you want *me* to produce *Much Ado* for you?'

'You're getting it right.' She had to hand it to him, he caught her drift, in the end.

'Who's playing the lead parts?'

'What's that got to do with anything?'

'You've asked me a favour, Erinna. Before I can answer, I need to know a few details.'

'As it happens,' she admitted, feeling strangely nervous, 'I've been asked to play Beatrice.'

'I see.' Had he been expecting that? Would it make any difference? Now he was frowning, turning to gaze out of the window. 'Am I fantasising, or do I seem to recall Becky mentioning something about that part?'

'You're not fantasising. She was going to play it, till she got ill.'

'And then they asked you to step into the breach.' He swung round to face her again. 'And Benedick?'

'Er...Anthony Travers.' For some reason, Erinna found herself muttering the name down to her clasped hands.

John's expression was particularly quizzical—too shrewd by a long way. 'And was it Anthony who asked you to put this "great favour" to me?'

'Yes, but on behalf of the whole...'

'Of course, of course.' John seemed plunged into meditation, staring into a far corner, then at the ceiling, anywhere but at Erinna.

'They—we couldn't think of anyone more suitable. I mean, with such a reputation, and your detailed knowledge of Shakespeare, especially the comedies. All those books you've written about them. You'd do it brilliantly. Please, Dr Bryce!'

She was too intelligent to think that flattery would cut any ice with this man. She meant the compliments, every syllable of them, and her tone said so. As she spoke, she lifted both hands in a pleading gesture. She was sure he registered it, out of the corner of an eye, but he went on surveying the middle distance, as if seeking inspiration from outside himself—or perhaps far inside.

Just as she was abandoning hope, he confronted her again. His tone and expression were peculiarly harsh. 'I don't know what to say. You've really put me on the spot, haven't you?'

'I didn't mean to.' But she sensed a move towards victory, and took blatant advantage of it. 'I do realise you don't like to involve yourself in University affairs much, Dr Bryce. No one blames you for that, or for preferring not to fraternise with us students. I dare say most of us are...' she swallowed the sarcastic phrase 'beneath your notice', and substituted '...not your usual choice of companion.'

John was not fooled. 'It's nothing to do with students, Erinna. I have little more truck with my colleagues on the staff. I make no real distinction between one person and another, on ageist grounds. I'm not too much given to—what was your word?—fraternising in general.'

'I only meant...' This was turning out even trickier than she'd dreaded. 'It might be nice if you took an active role in one of the college activities. You know, participated for a...'

'For a change?' he suggested, as she trailed off.

'Well, I didn't mean it that way, just...'

'Are you insinuating that I don't earn my keep here?'

'Of course not!' His hostility was so controlled, but that only made it the more daunting. Erinna cringed, but she kept her voice steady.

'So, who is?'

'No one is!' She bit her lip, remembering the Union bar chat which had hinted at precisely that.

'I should hope not.'

There was a painful pause, then Erinna took her courage in both hands and tried again. 'What should I tell them, Dr Bryce?'

'Don't I have time to consider your proposition?' He was sardonic now. 'Does the golden honour evaporate—

change into a pumpkin—if I don't commit myself by midday today?'

Erinna sighed. 'Of course, if you need time to think it over...'

'It's all right, I understand. They need to know, naturally.' Now he was being brisk and reasonable. Talk about paradoxes and contradictions! 'Well, I've thought it over, and I'm flattered to be asked, but no. I don't think I can accept, I'm sorry.'

'Oh.' She had to duck her head, to hide her sheer mortification.

'I'm sorry, Erinna, really. I'm a busy man, and I have...'

'You have no obligation to explain.' Erinna was already rallying from the blow. She never resorted to whining or grovelling. If the stuck-up Bryce refused to direct the play, someone else would have to be found. He might be the most eminent fish in this particular sea, but he needn't think he was unique or indispensable.

'Listen to me, Erinna. I'm trying to tell you, it's not that I wouldn't enjoy the experience. I know that, because I've had a fair bit to do with live theatre in my time, and...'

'So we understood.'

'But I do have other—there are reasons why it might prove problematical. For a start, I'm not always here. I have to go away...'

'That wouldn't have mattered,' Erinna said. 'We'd have fitted in our rehearsals around your demanding schedule.'

He chose to ignore her irony. 'It's more complicated than that. I'd prefer not to take it on, that's all.'

'You don't have to justify yourself. I asked you, and you gave me your reply, and that's fine. I respect your decision, even if I don't understand it. I'll tell Anthony tonight. They'll be disappointed, of course, but I'm sure they'll survive.'

She picked up her bag and briefcase. This time her exit would be as poised as it had been tempestuous last time. Her gaze moved from John's face to the window, then to the bookshelf and that row of shiny paperbacks. Suddenly, she looked straight at John and smiled.

'I bet you can't tell me what the names Devin O'Connor mean?'

'Mean?' John seemed utterly blank, as if she'd left him way behind.

'Yes, literally, mean. In English.'

His brows arched. 'I have a strong suspicion you're about to enlighten me.'

'I looked them up once. I've got this thing about names. Devin means swarthy poet. Connor means high desire.'

'You don't say so.' Her grin was so wide, it magnetised a trace of one from him. 'Swarthy poet of high desire, no less?'

'Can you imagine it, being called something so—so apt? He was fated, destined from birth to be what he is! Christened that, how could he be anything else?'

'He might not be swarthy,' John pointed out, rational as ever. Then he ran a hand through his hair, smiling at her, tangibly relaxing. 'What about *your* name? It's un-usual—presumably Irish, too?'

'Through and through,' she assured him promptly. 'Erinna means peace. Casey means brave. Should be a useful combination.'

John Bryce hesitated, and then, unbelievably, erupted into a peal of laughter. 'Useful? I should say so! But peace?'

Erinna fixed him with her most piercing glare. 'You find it funny?'

'Oh, come on, Erinna! Brave, I can accept. Brave suits you fine. Anyway, that's your surname, and I'm sure all your tribe are as—what shall we say—spirited as you are? But peace?' He was practically doubled up with mirth.

'I'm glad you find it so entertaining.'

Erinna was having a rare and real struggle not to dissolve in tears. John Bryce's amusement at her expense was extraordinarily cutting. She'd never felt so painful, or exposed. Was she really such a harridan, a harpy? Some kind of virago, always on the warpath? Was it really so ironic, her name meaning peace? She had always been proud of it; what's more, she had always regarded herself as kind and tender at heart, under the articulate flow of words—that armoury of language. This reaction, from this man, undermined her self-respect and shook her self-confidence in quite a new way.

Probably sensing this, he immediately stopped laughing. Then he took a step towards her. She tightened her grip on the chair-back, aware that her cheeks were burning.

'I'm sorry, Erinna. I didn't mean to upset you.'

'I'm not upset.'

'Or offend you.'

'I'm not offended.'

'All the same, I'm sorry.' He shook his head and moved another step closer. She stood her ground, grateful for the barrier of the chair. 'Erinna?' Before she could dodge or stiffen, he was reaching out a hand and laying it on her shoulder. The firm touch, and its effect, were paralysing. She went hot, then cold, then rigid all over, as if he had plugged her into a live socket.

'I didn't mean to hurt you. I don't generally laugh at people.' She had never heard his voice so soft; it was like a distortion of its usual dry self. 'It's not my way;

I've never liked it. But there was something about how you said it—I don't know, the timing...'

She raised her head, resolved to face him on equal terms. He already had so many of the advantages: age, status, wisdom—if you could call it that—experience...and, yes, and gender, when it came to plain brute strength if nothing else. She wasn't letting him get away with this old trick as well. Creeping round her with sweet talk and bodily contact...

'It's perfectly all right, Dr Bryce. I wasn't in the least bit hurt. I'm not that weak and pathetic. And I suppose it is rather a joke, when you come to think about it,' she lied bravely. Then she moved away, just far enough to make sure he dropped his hand. 'And now you'll have to excuse me.' She was gathering herself together again fast. 'What's the Yeats line everyone knows? "I will arise and go now..." I think we're safe with that one.' She attempted a light laugh.

John stared at her, then glanced at his watch and cleared his throat. 'You're right. My next class should be here.' He turned and retreated behind his desk, where he started sorting through files and books as if his sanity depended on it.

Erinna slung her coat round her shoulders—wishing one of them would stop tingling—and walked to the door. From there, she sent him a businesslike wave.

'I'll see you at the seminar on Thursday, then. *Tamburlaine the Great*, I think we're doing?'

'That's right. The way Marlowe deals with power and pride, in his...'

'*Hubris*,' Erinna interrupted, more to herself than to John. An excellent word, hubris, coined by the Greeks to mean insolent pride and over-confidence. A useful word, to describe certain individuals not a hundred miles from this room. Haughtiness, delusions of grandeur...

'Goodbye, Dr Bryce,' she said, turning the handle.

'Goodbye, Erinna,' he called. 'I'm...'

But she had already closed the door quietly behind her.

CHAPTER FOUR

IN HER own room, nearly nine hours later, Erinna sat cross-legged on her narrow bed, while Lisa occupied the one armchair.

'Oh, come on, Erinna! I'll buy you a drink. My grant came through at last today, so I feel generous.'

'Honestly, Lisa, it's the last thing I feel like. I mean, I haven't exactly got cause for celebration, have I? And I've got a heap of reading to do.'

'But you've been working for hours, you'll have to stop some time!' Lisa assumed her counselling voice. 'Look, we both know that's not why you won't come out. It's because you can't face the gorgeous Travers.'

Erinna grinned, rueful. 'No fooling you, is there?'

'But he'll have to know eventually! You did say you'd tell him this evening, and you can't keep the poor guy on tenterhooks!'

'He'd rather be on tenterhooks than know the awful truth,' Erinna moaned.

'But it isn't *your* fault Dr Bryce refused! At least you tried, and we all expected it, really. With his track record, it would have been pretty amazing if he'd accepted, wouldn't it? I'm sure Anthony...'

'Anthony was counting on me. The whole Dramsoc was counting on me,' Erinna lamented. 'Bloody Bryce! Who does he think he is?'

Lisa was an old hand at dealing with her friend's minor explosions. 'He knows exactly who he is, and what he's prepared to take on, Erinna. You can't blame him for being straight with you. It's none of our business if he prefers to keep his distance from...'

'Stop being so *rational*! You sound like him!'

Lisa came over to stand by the bed. 'I ought to be off. Won't you come? Really?'

'I might see you later, when I've—got myself together.'

'Got hyped up to break the news to Anthony, you mean?'

Erinna groaned. 'Oh, God, he's going to hate me!'

'Don't talk such twaddle! If that was all it took to make him hate you, you wouldn't want his friendship in the first place. Would you?' Lisa sat on the edge of the bed, peering intently into Erinna's face.

Erinna turned away, knowing her cheeks were pink. 'You don't like Anthony much, do you, Lisa?'

'I don't know him,' Lisa replied promptly. 'He doesn't let anyone very far in, does he, under that beautiful exterior?'

'You think his charms are only skin-deep. You think I'm immature and shallow, to be so crazy about him.'

'I didn't say that. I'll admit I don't...I'm not sure...' Lisa was making the effort to balance honesty with tact. 'I'm not quite sure I trust him, but I can't tell you why, either.'

'Just because he has this extrovert image and he's a brilliant actor, and incredibly good-looking, people think he can't be a nice person! Why shouldn't someone be attractive all the way through, not just on the surface? Why do you have to be so—so prejudiced?'

Lisa sighed, but she was smiling. 'Oh, Erinna, you never do anything by halves! I sometimes wonder why you seem to...'

'Seem to what?' Erinna snapped, as Lisa paused for thought.

'Seem to set your sights on goals that are obviously unattainable.'

'What makes you think that Anthony's unattainable?'

'Well, he's so careful to keep himself separate and single, isn't he? He never seems to have anyone specific, though there are plenty of hangers-on—groupies, Colin calls them.'

'Colin's just jealous, like most of the men,' Erinna declared. 'And the fact that Anthony chooses not to have serious girlfriends doesn't make him unattainable. Quite the opposite, surely? He just hasn't met the right female yet—or realised he has—that's all!'

Lisa pondered. 'Suppose you did succeed in arousing Anthony's interest? I mean, *real* interest?'

'If only I could!' Erinna's eyes were a green dream.

'That's what all this Beatrice and Benedick business is about, isn't it?' Lisa brought things down to brass tacks.

'Only partly!' But Erinna's denial lacked conviction.

'Oh, you genuinely want to act in the play, but if it wasn't for starring opposite Anthony...' Lisa waited for further protests, but they failed to come, so she continued. 'So let's say you showed signs of being Ms Right for Anthony, what would you do?'

'Do? Jump for joy, I should think!'

'I'm serious, Erinna. What usually happens, when you fancy some chap, pull out all the stops, exercise all your feminine wiles, and in the end he crumbles—putty in your hands? Or even shows the first signs of...'

'I do know what you're saying, Lisa.' Erinna's tone was flat and tense. 'As soon as I look like achieving my aim, I go off the whole idea. A man stops being the one I want, the big deal, as soon as he starts wanting *me*. If it all gets too easy, I lose the motivation.' She stared into space for a few seconds, before adding, 'I've always been like this, ever since I grew up. It's something to do with...'

'Exactly. We've all watched it happen, at least three times these last two years. So why should it be any different with Anthony?'

'It *is* different. I don't know how, Lisa, but I'm sure it is.'

Lisa looked dubious. 'You said that before, remember, with...?'

'No,' Erinna cut in, decisive now. 'Under that polished veneer, he's a great person, I sense it. If I could only find a way through to the real him...the real Anthony!'

'You generally do. Then, when there's the remotest chance of hooking the poor guy, you'll change your mind and call the whole thing off!' Lisa sat back with the air of a lawyer completing a cast-iron case.

'I know that's what I've tended to do before. It won't be like that this time.' For Erinna, this reaction was positively humble.

'If you say so, love!' Lisa stood up again. 'Look, I really must go. I said I'd be there at eight, and you know how jittery Mike gets if we're ten minutes late; he thinks everyone's deserted him.' She picked up her jacket, then swung to face Erinna. 'Now there's a case in point.'

'Mike, you mean?'

'Mike, I mean.'

Erinna scowled, half wistful, half irritated. 'I'm fond of Mike, Lisa, just as we all are. He's a lovely bloke, really sweet, a good mate and...'

'And nuts about you.' Lisa hovered, as if poised for a speedy getaway.

But still the attack did not come. Erinna was really subdued tonight. That gruelling session with the uncom-

promising Bryce must have deflated her even more than
she was letting on.

'I realise that,' she muttered now. 'But what can I do
about it? Talk about being unattainable…Mike's trouble
is, he's only too available! Anyway, even if he wasn't, I
don't fancy him. He's not my type, so—so young, and
solemn, and transparent. I like him a lot, but not that
way.'

'It's all right, you don't need to go into such stric-
tures!' Lisa was grinning. 'I'd feel the same myself, if
it was me he lusted after!'

'Lusted after? That's a bit strong, isn't it? I mean…'

'Oh, don't be so coy! Isn't that what it all comes down
to, in the end—the call of the flesh?' Lisa was not without
some worldly wisdom in these matters. At twenty-four,
she was a couple of years older than most Finalists, and
a year older than Erinna.

'There's a damn sight more to it than just sex, and
you know it!' Now Erinna *did* get steamed up. 'Actually, what you're saying about Mike is that he's quite
like me. A romantic. For us, the searching is more important and valuable than the finding. We need a target
to strive for, even pine for. I may be one of his pals, but
that's still how he looks at me—I recognise the
symptoms. If I ever suddenly returned his feelings, or
what he thinks are his feelings, he'd almost certainly run
a mile in the other direction.'

'Just as you do,' Lisa observed. 'Safer that way, isn't
it?'

'OK, you've made your point! But I still say it's not
like that with Anthony. Which brings us back to tonight's small problem.'

Lisa slipped her jacket on, and arranged the collar
neatly. 'And *I* still say you should come out with me
and get it over with. He'll be expecting you. In fact,

Erinna, he might come looking for you here, if he doesn't see you in the Union. After all, you did say you'd...'

'He wouldn't, would he?' But in her secret heart, Erinna was half hoping for just that. It might be easier to deal with a sad and disappointed Anthony alone, one to one, without the constant attendants he collected in public places. Just for once, it might even give her a chance to strip off a few layers—figuratively, of course— and get to know him better. Or at least encourage him to get to know *her*, so...

'I doubt it. Anthony needs his audience.' Lisa was too acute for comfort, but she was loyal and level-headed, and Erinna appreciated her concern. 'Still, you never know. This time it might just be vital enough for him to beard you in your den.'

'I'll have to take the risk.' But Erinna leaped from the bed and began brushing out her gloriously tangled mane, as if she expected him to materialise. 'If you see him, tell him I'll be along soon, OK?'

'OK. Presumably you'd prefer me not to tell him anything else?'

'The outcome of this morning's fiasco, you mean?' Erinna hesitated. It was tempting to let Lisa do her dirty work, but she owed Anthony a direct account of Bryce's reaction; and to be truthful she'd rather enjoy delivering it, in her best histrionic style. She wasn't above playing to the gallery herself, especially if Anthony Travers happened to be in the front row.

'No, I'll speak to him myself,' she said. 'In my own way and my own time. I'm sure we can find a substitute director, and I want him to be sure, too. I'm determined this show's going to go ahead, and be a success, if I have anything to do with it.'

Lisa knew this Erinna, too: the proud toss of the head, the stubborn tilt of the chin, the gleam in the eyes.

'That's the spirit, love! Show Bryce he ain't the only pebble on the beach. Well, more of a boulder, really, but there must be one or two more of those about too, if you know where to look.'

'A boulder, that's great!' Erinna chuckled, putting down her hairbrush. 'And of course he's not unique; that's just what I thought, after he showed me the door.' She pulled her sweatshirt off over her shining head. The last half-hour had seen a meteoric swoop from depression to optimism, fully in character, but disconcerting unless you understood her.

Lisa understood her. 'Right, so have a wash and change, and you'll be ready to tackle Anthony. Just remember you did all you could. He can't eat you.'

'I should be so lucky!' Erinna was as energised as she had just been listless, charging about her room, rummaging through drawers and cupboards for the right outfit, designed to boost self-confidence and inspire admiration in certain quarters.

'That's better.' Lisa decided to escape, before she was flattened in Erinna's dash for the bathroom. 'See you a bit later, then.'

'See you, Lisa! And thanks!' Erinna called, as her friend shut the door.

Fifteen minutes later, refurbished in full navy skirt, soft patterned sweater and short boots, Erinna was addressing her reflection in the wardrobe mirror, rehearsing possible approaches to this unenviable task ahead.

'What I thought, Anthony, was that if we...it may be a blessing in disguise, Anthony, because...Dr Bryce is such a tricky customer to pin down, you see, Anthony, whereas...had you considered asking one of your own tutors? After all, they must be...'

The knock on her door was short and sharp, alien and unfamiliar. Not one of her regular visitors, she was sure.

Anthony! It must be! As Lisa had predicted, he'd grown bored of waiting in the Union and come to find out the verdict for himself. Well, she was ready—externally, at least.

'Come in!' She opened the door with a flourish.

The man on her threshold did not obey her invitation, but then, he was not Anthony. He was in direct contrast to Anthony in almost every respect. Instead of being fair, smooth and smiling, he was dark, stern and rugged. Instead of sporting the latest in baggy trousers and eye-catching pullovers, he wore plain, lean jeans and a Guernsey sweater.

They did have one feature in common at this moment, however. Anthony had recently been affecting a crop of blond designer stubble, carefully nurtured. This person, now confronting Erinna, was no tender youth, but a man in his prime. Clearly the kind of man who needed to shave twice a day, and equally clearly one whose face hadn't seen a razor since first thing this morning. In this case, the resulting shadow was there by accident, not design, indicating rush, preoccupation, a mind on higher matters, or...

'Good evening, Erinna.'

'Dr Bryce!' She stood back, one hand flying to her mouth, dumbfounded. 'What are *you* doing here? Why? How?'

'No mystery about how. The location of rooms in our residential halls is no state secret on this campus.' He still did not smile, but he stood at ease, arms folded, feet slightly apart. 'As to why, if I could come in for a few minutes, there's no mystery about that either.'

'Oh, I'm sorry. It's just that you took me by surprise...'

She stood aside to let him in, then closed the door behind him. He looked her up and down before demanding, 'Expecting someone, were you?'

'No, nothing like that. I was on my way out to meet some of the others. Won't you—won't you sit down?' She indicated the chair, then perched on the edge of her rumpled bed, flustered, embarrassed.

'Won't keep you long—wouldn't want to disrupt you.' He made himself comfortable, stretching his legs and crossing them at the ankles, linking his hands behind his head as he assessed the untidy room.

Disrupt her? What was the man playing at now? He, of all people, who never encouraged social contact with students, let alone went out of his way to penetrate their domain? Erinna waited, for once lost for appropriate words.

'Not bad, is it?' he was observing. 'Cosy and well furnished.'

'It's no different from all the others.'

'I haven't been in any of the others,' he replied evenly. 'But I can see you've made it distinctive, left your mark on it.'

'We all try to do that.' Distinctive was one word for this shambles of books and folders strewn over the desk and parts of the floor; clothes draped on most surfaces; walls festooned with lists and letters, messages and cuttings, pin-ups ranging from Marlon Brando to Mel Gibson.

'And at least it's warm.' He pulled his heavy sweater over his head and deposited it on the floor without ceremony. Erinna tried not to stare at the way his short, dark hair was left standing on end by this vigorous gesture, and the collar of his check shirt turned up. He did not notice—and if he had, he wouldn't have cared.

'Er—I could offer you a cup of coffee, but it would mean going down to the...'

'No, thanks, Erinna. I've just had a drink.'

She glanced sharply at him. One drink, or several? Surely not fortifying himself to confront her? She shifted uneasily, tucking her legs up under her, a favourite position. 'That's all right, then.' This small talk only made her feel more tense. One did not indulge in small talk with John Bryce. 'So, what was it you...?'

He brought his hands down hard on his knees, as if to focus his own concentration. Then he smiled. As always, it was powerfully unexpected.

'I know I said you must have had enough of me for one day, but it seems you haven't got rid of me yet. I've been thinking things through since this morning, and I've realised I was wrong. I wanted to tell you, as soon as possible. That's why I'm here.'

The infallible Bryce, admitting to error, or misjudgement? But thinking *what* through? There had been more than one clash of wills this morning, as Erinna recalled only too vividly.

'Wanted to tell me what?' she ventured.

He leaned forward now, hands still resting on his knees. She noticed them for the first time: interesting hands, chunky, capable, unadorned—but sensitive in the way he used them, the way they were often on the move, reinforcing a point. Perhaps even expressing a feeling? Yes, he probably expressed more with his hands than his voice; a sobering idea.

But he was speaking earnestly now, and the hands remained motionless, as if providing an anchorage for that calm control he specialised in.

'First, let me ask you a question, Erinna. About this play.'

'*Much Ado*, you mean?' So, they were back to that subject?

'That's the one. When is it due to be performed?'

'After Easter. I'm not sure how long after we get back from the spring holiday, but some time in late April I should think. Why?'

'Don't you think that's cutting it a bit fine with your exams?'

'My exams?' So that was it! He was here to ensure that his star candidate wasn't about to jeopardise her chances by channelling vital energy into amateur theatricals! This was no personal visit, but a professional one, from tutor to student; paternalistic, authoritarian.

'I know a major part of your degree is already confirmed through ongoing work. But I hope you haven't forgotten how crucial those papers in June are, Erinna? You won't get your First without doing well in them.'

'I'm aware of that, Dr Bryce.' Unusually, she exercised even more quiet self-discipline than he did. 'I had taken it into my calculations. I do happen to be concerned about the outcome of my Finals. Amazing though it may seem, possibly even more concerned than you are.'

'Don't get me wrong, Erinna, it's not that I don't trust you. It's just that I can see how tempting it would be, the prospect of acting such a great role in such a great piece—especially to you.'

'Why especially to me?'

'Because you love Shakespeare. Because you have a true comprehension of what he says and how he says it. Not many people do, in my experience, including some who purport to.'

'Oh.' A backhanded compliment, if ever she had received one! 'So, as my tutor, you deplore my decision to take this on, but defend to the death my right to decide? Is that it?'

'Not exactly.' The more prickly she grew, the more he relaxed. 'As long as you've really considered it—all the implications. I know you'd never willingly let your work slip, but I also know how absorbing these productions can be, and how exhausting. For your own sake, I felt it my duty to...I wouldn't want you to...' He lifted both hands, palms up.

'Bite off more than I can chew?' Erinna was starchier than ever. 'It's kind of you, Dr Bryce, and I appreciate that you have my best interests at heart, but I assure you it won't make the slightest difference to my performance when it comes to Finals. I'll have weeks, after it's all over, for recuperation and revision. Also,' she pointed out, 'I do know practically all of Beatrice's lines already—Benedick's too, come to that—we did study it together, didn't we? You can't explore Shakespeare in depth without the best bits rubbing off in your mind.'

'*You* might not be able to.' John was wry. 'With most of my students, it hardly touches the sides.'

Despite her irritation, Erinna was intrigued. There was something new about him tonight, but what? Less guarded, less formal? Perhaps to do with being on her patch rather than his own; perhaps he felt there was less expected of him here, less front to maintain than facing her from behind desk or lectern?

The trouble with sitting on her folded legs was that she got pins and needles in them. Now she moved them out and planted her feet primly on the floor.

'I hope that sets your mind at rest then, Dr Bryce?'

'I had to make the point. Now that's out of the way— I made it, you dealt with it, I accept your assurances, so that's fine.'

He made it sound so theoretical, like one of their literary arguments. 'It might be fine, if we happened to have a producer of the right calibre.'

'Yes, and that's the main reason I'm here.'

Erinna sat bolt upright, her eyes wide. 'You've thought of someone else? You've got another suggestion?' The stiffness had miraculously melted, and she was all agog.

'I've reconsidered my position. I know you didn't ask me to, Erinna. I suspect that's why I did.' He smiled. 'I've been thinking about it all day and I've decided to take it on, after all.'

'You'll *do* it? You'll direct the play?'

She was on her feet now, so that he had to look up at her. 'If you still want me to.'

'*Want* you to? You have to be joking!' She could not have smothered her broad grin, even if she'd tried. This time, Bryce had excelled himself; this time he'd really confounded her! And the news was as timely as it was incredible. Thank goodness she hadn't got round to telling Anthony! He was going to be so pleased. She couldn't wait to see his...

'That's OK, then.' John was watching her closely.

'OK? It's wonderful! I can't thank you enough! You're an angel! I don't know what made you change your mind, but I'm glad it did!'

Suddenly John was standing too, six inches taller than Erinna, and not much further away. 'I'm no angel, believe me. Flesh and blood, like anyone else. And nothing *made* me change my mind. *I* changed it.'

His voice dropped now, low and intense. He stood so close, but she could easily have backed away. For some reason she stayed put, half hypnotised like a cornered prey.

'I'd better go now, Erinna. You'll be wanting to spread the word.'

'They'll be so pleased, Dr Bryce. They'll want me to...'

He seemed to reach an instant decision. 'Look, Erinna, if we're going to be mutually involved in this project, I think it's time you dropped the Dr Bryce bit. My name is John. Please feel free to start using it. All of you, that is. I prefer to operate as a unit in a team, not some tinpot dictator on a pedestal.'

Erinna stared; she couldn't help herself. He was really coming up with them tonight! 'But we thought you hated being treated as...'

'An equal?' He was ready for this one. 'It's not that at all. It's perfectly simple—over the years I've found it best to keep a distance between staff and under-graduates.'

'Best academically, or personally?' she challenged, taking herself by surprise, the moment the words were out.

'Academically, of course.' But he smiled, adding to the surprise. 'Well, maybe a bit of both.'

'So what's the difference, if you're directing a play?'

'A lot of difference, you must see that? I've just told you I'll consider myself one part of a democratic group, not in my role as tutor. So, please tell the others to cut the formalities and honour me with my given name. Dull and commonplace though it may be,' he added with a quick grin.

'John's a good name,' Erinna found herself declaring. 'Just because it's not rare or exotic, like—like mine, or...'

'Or Devin, for instance?' His smile widened, and he seemed to draw closer, though she could swear he never actually moved a muscle.

Then, completely without warning, he half turned and picked up the paperback which lay open, face down, on

her desk. The collected Devin O'Connor. She'd forgotten it was there, and he'd shown no sign of noticing.

'I was reminding myself of some of his poems, after
today's tutorial.' No explanations were necessary, of
course, but she felt ridiculously bare, exposed, as he
flicked the pages of the book, frowning.

Suddenly he was handing it to her. 'Let's hear you
read this.'

'Why?' And why was she trembling?

'If I'm going to direct you in Shakespeare, I might as
well hear how you sound when you're declaiming. In
public, that is; I've heard plenty in private!' He smiled
again. 'Anyway, presumably O'Connor intends his stuff
to be delivered in Irish cadences. You've got just the
voice.'

Erinna stared down at the page, although she knew
every word by heart. Without bothering to clear the slight
huskiness from her throat, she launched into the simple
little verses he had chosen.

> '''I had a little apple tree, and it was all I had,
> The blossoms they were beautiful, the apples all
> were bad.
> I had a little story book, and it was all I had,
> The stories they were sweetly told, and all of them
> were sad.
> I had a little lover once, and she was all I had,
> Her heart it filled with love for me, and burst,
> and drove her mad.
> I had a little life on earth, and it was all I had,
> And though it sent me only death, I lived it and
> was glad.'''

Then she waited in silence, still staring at the page.
When John said nothing, she raised her head. He was

apparently deep in contemplation of his shoes, so she risked a cautious comment.

'A fine use of ballad form, I always think. Deceptively simple, but with subtle undertones. Mind you, I think I prefer his more...'

'Beautifully read!' John interrupted briskly. 'I think we should keep a Celtic Beatrice. With your colouring—yes, I think you should give a Beatrice just like that!'

She was still steeped in the poem. 'Never mind the way I read it! What about the poem itself?'

'Oh, it's quite clever in its way, but I tend to go more for his less sentimental ones. He does a good line in political satire, if I remember rightly, in among all that soul-searching. Titles like Emerald I'll, and Crème De La Kremlin.'

'But this isn't sentimental! It's...'

John reached out and took the book from her grasp, replacing it on the desk. 'Call it what you will—tragic, romantic, pathetic. Let's not go into all that again, Erinna, for God's sake!'

'No. I'm sorry, Dr Bryce.'

'John,' he corrected.

'John,' she whispered obediently. This was no time to land on the wrong side of him again, not after what he'd just agreed to do.

'It's only words on paper, you know. Clever use of language, imagery, some orchestration of feeling, but not the real thing. Only a two-dimensional representation of it.'

He seemed edgy now. She gazed at him in astonishment. *Feeling?* What did he know about *the real thing*? 'But Dr Bryce...'

'*John,*' he insisted.

'John,' she muttered. It was agitating, using his first name—like crashing through a safety barrier. Such an ordinary, everyday name, in fact, she used it most days on more than one of her acquaintances; but it felt extra-ordinary, even illicit, to be using it on him.

'Erinna, a word of advice.' He was definitely keyed-up now, boiling to purge something from his system. Some overflow, aimed at her, she could sense that—and not at her intellect, but the soft, vulnerable layers near the centre. There was no deflecting him, so she braced herself. 'For such an intelligent woman, you have a re-markable tendency to confuse fantasy with reality. We've discussed it in literature, of course, several times over the last few months, but if we're going to work together on *Much Ado* as well as the rest, it's important that you learn to recognise it, because...'

Erinna was struggling to keep her cool, but it had never been so difficult. '*A remarkable tendency,* have I? You know me so well, do you?'

'I know you better than you think. Our discussions, and your written offerings, can be highly revealing.' He was clearly heating up, himself, despite a determination to stay calm.

'Oh, yes? Highly revealing, can they?'

He sighed heavily. 'Look, I didn't mean this to happen. I'm not trying to undermine you. Don't take it the wrong way.'

'Is there a right way?' She was only vaguely aware that she was squaring up to him, like a boxer.

'Since we've got this far...' He held out a hand, as if to bridge a spreading gulf between them. 'Acting in plays, especially romantic parts like Beatrice, could have intrinsic dangers for a person like you. One can get so immersed in the world of the imagination, especially when it's brought to life by a master of language and psychology...'

'Such as Shakespeare?' she snapped.

'Or Yeats, or any other craftsman. I've watched the close interaction between you and poetry, as well as you and drama, on the page. I can guess how intense your responses might be on the stage.'

'Oh, you can guess, can you? Clever old you!'

He was still holding his own temper under careful rein, but only just. It was foolhardy, defying him like this when so much else was at stake, but it carried an odd exhilaration, and anyway, she was genuinely angry.

'All I'm saying, Erinna, is there's a real world out there, and it doesn't do to become too steeped in a fantasy one. People are real, feelings are real, relationships are real, not just notions in your head—or mine, or...' he shrugged '...or Devin O'Connor's. Whoever you like. Not just idealised figures in an idealised landscape. Not some romantic dream, but *real*!'

Erinna literally could not believe what she was hearing—and from whom. '*You* talk about people and feelings being real! Of all the...'

Before she could spell out her opinion of him and his pretensions, he changed gear, tipped over an edge, from words to actions.

'A real world...real people...real feelings...' He went on muttering, becoming less coherent as he leaned closer. 'You think you know all about human nature and emotions, Erinna...you think you can judge from appearances, but you don't know the half—the quarter—the tiniest fraction of it. Never mistake illusion for the thing itself.'

Currents of rage mingled with amazement, then anticipation. Then, as his mouth sought and found hers, a pure, profound, physical shock.

It was a light kiss, but not tentative. A kiss that knew precisely what it was saying and where it was heading.

A long, subtle exploration; a positive statement, not a question.

She felt his lips, his tongue, the rasp of rough skin on smooth; heard his deepened breathing and the pounding of her own pulse inside her ears. The sensations were in her, and all round her—happening to her, yet separate from her. It had always been like this, with such intimate contact. The immediate escape, the stepping outside reality, into a secure distance, opting out...

Was John Bryce right, after all? Did he, by some mysterious osmosis, know her better than she knew herself?

When he drew back at last, she registered for the first time how heavy his hands were on her shoulders, fingers biting through the soft wool of her jumper. Even so, she could have pulled away, but she did not try. She stared up into his clear grey eyes. Her own were glistening, bright but bewildered.

'Fantasy or reality?' he murmured, smiling now. 'Where do they begin? Where do they end? Who's going to say?'

For once in her life, Erinna was not going to. John was moving in again, his expression and tone hardening as he demanded, 'Wouldn't you rather have the real thing, Erinna, than all the stirring phrases and images in all the poems on earth?'

She closed her eyes. This time there was no anger or surprise, only a new surge of acute pleasure as his lips touched hers again. This time her mouth opened at once under the pressure of his, as he gathered her against him—hard against his body, making his own claim on reality without need of words.

This time the messages were filtering through, and she gasped, reeling, bending backwards—caving in, dissolving under that passionate demand. And giving, for the first time ever—returning, in full measure, what she was being offered—the sharpest reality of all.

It seemed the knock on her door came from another dimension. Not her door at all, but miles away, in another corridor, another building, another life...

But it came again, and a male voice called at the same time, 'Erinna?'

They broke apart, instinctively guilty. John turned aside, running a hand through his tousled hair. Erinna backed away, evading his influence several minutes too late.

She knew who this intruder was. He had never been to her room before, either, but there was a perfect, logical irony in his arrival here at this moment. The whole situation had a reality all of its own.

She crossed to the door, glancing at John over her shoulder, brows raised. He nodded briefly: permission, or resignation? It seemed to Erinna that they were cementing a conspiracy, whichever it was.

She opened the door, finding her most welcoming smile from somewhere. 'Anthony!' Her voice was creditably steady. 'I was all set to come out and find you!'

'Hi!' Anthony sauntered in, gazing round but only half seeing. 'I came to ask if you've managed to nail the dreaded...ah!' His eye lit on John, now leaning on Erinna's desk, arms folded. 'Dr Bryce!' he went on, so fluently you could hardly hear the join. 'I didn't realise!'

'Dr Bryce just dropped by to say he'll direct the play, Anthony. Isn't that marvellous?'

'Fantastic!' Anthony's delight was sincere. 'Thank you very much, sir! We're truly grateful. We...'

'John,' amended John breezily, waving Anthony's gratitude away. Presented with this scenario, he was as dour as Erinna had seen him—grim, turned inside-out in the space of a minute.

Perhaps it was just as well Anthony had appeared when he did. After what had just happened, she wouldn't put it past John to change his mind back again. On all rational grounds, it would probably have been better if he had, but Erinna hadn't gone to all that trouble to pin him down, only to lose him. And now it was official, he couldn't retreat without losing face and credibility.

As soon as Anthony was ensconced in the room, John was making for the door. 'That's OK,' he stated tersely, in reply to Anthony's continuing protestations of gratitude. 'Let me know when you want to start rehearsals. I have a tight timetable, so we'll need to fix it up carefully.' At the door he turned, looking straight at Erinna for the first time since Anthony's arrival. 'See you Thursday, then, at the seminar.'

Before either of them could answer, he was gone. Erinna stared after him, conscious of the most paradoxical blend of relief and emptiness.

Anthony smiled and arched his eyebrows elegantly. 'Strange fellow, Bryce, I've always thought. Hey, well done, Erinna! Using your charms to full advantage!'

How much had he seen—or read into the situation? Erinna opened her mouth, but no suitable words emerged, so she shut it again.

'It's great news,' Anthony went on, fully restored to his confident self now that John was out of the way. 'We must have a drink to celebrate. Come on, Erinna, we've got to let the others know—they're all waiting in the bar, and the suspense is terrible, you can't imagine.'

He was already on his way to the door. Erinna stared at his back, still fighting off waves of conflict.

He really was unfairly, painfully attractive. And real— surely as real as any other man? Not some impossible dream? Not some figment of her own unfulfilled yearnings?

Grabbing her bag and coat, she followed him out of her room.

CHAPTER FIVE

"'I HAD rather hear my dog bark at a crow,'" snarled Erinna, stage left, "'than a man swear he loves me.'"

"'God keep your ladyship still in that mind,'" retorted Anthony scathingly, "'so some gentleman or other shall escape a predestinate scratched face!'"

"'Scratching could not make it worse, if it were such a face as yours were,'" taunted Erinna.

Anthony stepped back, folding his arms. "'Well, you are a rare parrot-teacher!'"

Erinna was razor-sharp. "'A bird of my tongue is better than a beast of yours!'" And she stuck her tongue out at him to prove it.

John Bryce sat alone in the auditorium. Third row back, slightly right of centre, his favoured position from which to observe and direct. There was no denying it, these two made a formidable team. Anthony shone as the handsome, debonair, witty Benedick, while Erinna was actually capturing Beatrice's marvellous, elusive quality—that sparkling intelligence, quicksilver femininity, combined with a softer wistfulness which she so nearly kept hidden. In Erinna's hands, Beatrice appeared as what John considered her to be: Shakespeare's most fascinating heroine.

It was Shakespeare, of course, who had written all that chemistry into the two characters. All the actors had to do was interpret the lines with some sensitivity, and the alchemy would happen for them. Anthony and Erinna both understood their roles well enough, so why should they have any trouble establishing that vital relationship?

John frowned, irritated with himself. There was more to it than that, as he well knew. This complex interaction between Beatrice and Benedick—this ancient, delectable, romantic blend of attraction with antagonism—depended on at least some affinity between their interpreters. On the face of it, Anthony and Erinna were compatible, an ideal couple. How things really stood between them, away from this arena of public work and emotion, John could only watch and guess.

As if by mutual consent, he and Erinna had avoided being alone together since that unfortunate lapse of self-control in her room. He still encountered her regularly at lectures and seminars; there was no getting out of that. But two new faces had appeared at their Monday sessions, transplanted from one of John's larger groups—two or three being the normal student complement at tutorials—which was just as well, in John's opinion. A few more weeks of undiluted Erinna, and he would have had to apply to have her transferred himself!

Now here they were, already at the fourth rehearsal, or was it the fifth? He had been so busy lately, with commitments here and elsewhere, he had lost count of the weeks. It must be the fifth; they were well into February, and all that dratted snow had finally gone, giving way to fierce frosts and serrated winds.

Two evenings a week, he relentlessly coached and coaxed this diverse band of young amateurs, determined to create a competent production out of them by April. Apart from the two stars, talent levels were not notably high. In fact, in some cases, mediocre might be a kind label. But it was too late for re-casting, and John prided himself on squeezing top results from unpromising material.

He focused his attention back to the platform, where there was a general, and hopelessly untidy, commotion.

'"Please it your Grace lead on?"' invited the Governor of Messina, standing aside politely so that two courtiers had to dodge out of the way.

'"Your hand, Leonato,"' Don Pedro protested, in gracious, princely tones. '"We will go together."'

The group began to shuffle inexpertly towards the wings.

'OK, OK!' John was on his feet, text in one hand, the other pointing energetically at the stage. 'Exeunt all but Benedick and Claudio—but can't you do it with more conviction? Look, you *know* what positions you should be in; we choreographed this bit last time. Don't tell me you've forgotten already? And I know there are a lot of you on stage at this point, but could you *please* try not to come over quite such a shambles? You look more like a crowd of Oxford Street window-shoppers than the dignified gentry of Messina. Hero, I do realise you haven't exactly had much to say yet . . .'

'One line,' muttered Hero gloomily.

'Well, your time will come, but meanwhile, for God's sake, stop drooping around like a wilting daffodil! We know you're supposed to be demure and self-effacing, compared to Beatrice, but at least show a hint of spirit! Remember—and this applies to everyone—you should be acting your socks off *all* the time, not just when you think you're in the limelight.'

'Sorry, John.' Hero bit her lip. He could be a proper tyrant, this Bryce, but he commanded real respect. He knew what he was about, that was for sure. Sometimes it seemed he was just ordering them around haphazardly, for the sake of it, and then suddenly the scene would click, and they understood where he had been leading all along.

Erinna came to the front of the stage. 'Was there something wrong just then?'

'Just when?' John pushed the dark hair from his brow, and glared coldly at his leading lady.

'A few lines back, where Benedick says...'

'I didn't stop you, did I?'

'No, but I saw you frown. I thought you seemed... disapproving.'

John frowned again, but converted it quickly to a smile. 'It must be your own self-critic in operation, Erinna. If I frowned, it was purely personal, probably reflex. When I have a comment to make, you may be sure I'll make it, loud and clear.'

'So I thought. That's why I was surprised when I happened to glance at you, and I noticed...'

'Erinna, your business is not to observe every flicker of my face. Your business is to concentrate on giving us a superb Beatrice. To listen to what she has to say, and what Shakespeare has to say, and then what I have to say—in that order. Then to act on all of them as well as you can.'

'I do know that.' Erinna confronted him calmly, hands shoved deep in the pockets of her striped dungarees. She knew him better than the others, she could afford to challenge him. 'It was just the way you...'

'How's it going, anyway?' Anthony had sauntered to join her. 'Are we getting some sense out of it, John?'

'We've got a long way to go yet.' John regarded him steadily. 'A whole lot more time and hard graft, from each one of us, and we just *might* knock a bit of shape into this show.'

Suddenly he was vaulting the two rows of seats, up across the footlights, to stand among them. 'Now, I've got one or two points to raise before we press on. First, Beatrice.' He swung round to face Erinna, now only a couple of feet away. 'Never forget this: you are *not* some shallow coquette, playing with words and feelings. Even at this early stage, we must catch a glimpse of your real personality. You are a woman of depth and integrity, faithfulness to those you love, moral determination. You are always truthful, it's your stock-in-trade. And you can only love a man who comes close to matching your own intellectual resource, your idea of what's true and false. All this verbal banter is just a front. Underneath, you hide a very different centre: sensitive and serious. You know yourself to be equal to any man, if not superior to most, but the society you live in doesn't allow you to do much about proving it. So you feel this nagging frustration, as well as everything else. You're essentially female and vulnerable, but you suffer this inner conflict which drives you to clash with the male you actually like and desire most.' John paused, drew a long breath, and raised his eyebrows. 'Got that?'

Throughout this diatribe, Erinna's green eyes had never left his. Her soft mouth remained firm and unsmiling. When he had finished, she nodded her bright head once, and said quietly, 'I think we established most of that in our tutorials, but thanks all the same for reminding me. I'm obviously not getting it quite right yet.'

'It can never do any harm to underline these things. And Beatrice is well worth getting right. She's by far the most complex character in this play, probably the most complex in Shakespeare, certainly among his women.' Abruptly, John switched his attention to Anthony, standing nearby, listening laconically along with the rest of the cast. 'Now, Benedick, let's sort out a few small points about *you...*'

At ten-thirty, half an hour late, he let them go. The caretaker was waiting to lock the hall, or he might well have kept them longer. John Bryce was a demanding taskmaster, demanding of himself as well as everyone else. His own students knew that already, and the members of Dramsoc were rapidly discovering it. Not just the action of the play, but the design—sets, costumes, lighting, music, every aspect of a successful piece of theatre—came under his intent scrutiny. No detail, plan or proposal escaped his quick ears and eyes.

It hadn't been like this with Julian Tench, but then Julian was hardly in the Bryce league. Some of the cast occasionally wondered whether they had bitten off more than they could chew, involving themselves with this man, but their pride in the production overcame any lurking doubts. He might be forceful, even ferocious, but he was generally fair, and away from the director's hot seat he was almost always friendly and personal. On the whole, they were pleased to have won him, grateful for his unique flair and precious time. All that experience and charisma could do nothing but good to their reputation.

Anthony, in particular, was delighted at how things were working out. Taking his leave now, he grinned and clapped John on the shoulder. 'Goodnight, then, John. Thanks for everything. Next week as usual?'

John winced privately at the matey gesture, but returned the smile. 'Should be fine, as far as I know. See you then, Anthony.'

The others filed round them, waving and smiling with shy nonchalance, determined to behave on equal terms with their director, when they knew full well they never could be.

'Cheers, Anthony,'

'Night, Dr Bryce—er, John.'

'See you.'

'Cheers...'

'Coming for a drink?' Erinna had been back to fetch her coat, and now she appeared beside Anthony, one arm threading itself through his. 'It must be nearly last orders, but if we hurry we could . . .'

Anthony's smile was radiant as he looked into her face. 'I'd love to, partner, but I can't tonight. I've got a whole file of notes to mug up for a seminar tomorrow. Another time, maybe?'

'Not even ten minutes?' Erinna, the consummate actress, kept her voice cool, but John Bryce was neither blind nor deaf to that underlying urgency.

'No, really, love. I'm just going to grab a coffee and lock myself in my room. Got this essay on Restoration Tragedy to produce by . . .'

'You work too hard. Rehearsals are exhausting. You should take some time off to relax after them, at least.' She made it sound flip, but her bitter disappointment was clear to John. It must surely have reached Anthony as well, but he gave no sign. He patted her hand where it lay on his arm, before extricating himself from her. His smile held a genuine warmth, yet it was unconvincing somehow, as if his goodwill was general, not aimed at Erinna in particular, as she obviously craved.

John had witnessed this little scene before. After each rehearsal, in fact, when Erinna made her brave bid to lead Anthony away to the Union, or anywhere as long as it was exclusively in her company. Each time, Anthony had refused, firmly but with a degree of charm. There was no other woman in evidence. Sometimes he went off alone, or more often with a group of friends, but always with something vital to do which did not necessarily include Erinna.

Up to now, Erinna had seemed to take his rebuffs in the right spirit, marching off with a cheery wave or running to catch up with the others as they headed for the bar. But this evening she was more upset—or less able to conceal it. Anthony buttoned his jacket as he bowed smoothly out.

'I know. Work, work, work...I'll drive myself into the ground one of these days. It shouldn't be allowed! Pity my tutors don't see it that way. See you both next week, and thanks again, John. It's all going really well. Cheers, Erinna!'

Then he was gone, out into the night, his jaunty step receding in the direction of the house-blocks. Unlike Erinna, who still chose to have an undergraduate room to herself, he shared a campus flat with three other Finalists.

Erinna and John, left alone in the doorway, stared at each other—just a few seconds, but long enough for John to read all her tension and dejection, before she pulled herself together and banished them. With a swift smile and a tremulous ''Night John!', she pushed open the door and slipped out.

The caretaker was advancing, meaningfully brandishing his bunch of keys, but John was on his way outside and shrugging into his coat as he followed Erinna. She had already merged into the icy darkness, but his acute hearing—or was it some subtler instinct?—received the sound of her agile footsteps on the concrete path. She was sprinting—beating her retreat, away from the Union, the residential halls, all the built-up part of the campus—towards the lake.

At the same time, that voice of intuition told John that she was sobbing her heart out.

The lake was one of the best features of this landscaped compound. Not far from the centre, just below the Senate house, past the main lecture theatres and the Vice Chancellor's office...take this short cut up over a green slope and down the other side to meet the lakeside track...

Erinna ran all the way, anorak flying open, hair streaming free. The cold air was soothing to her heated skin. Her flat shoes felt good, gliding on grass, crunching on gravel, then padding on half-frozen mud. The water lay silent and secret, a mysterious, spreading shadow, no longer iced over, but almost as solid and still as when it had been.

All that liquid, and now her tears fell fluently as if to swell it. This situation was so painfully unfair! These rehearsal sessions, so emotionally stimulating, as she and Anthony struck such perfect chords and discords... she could tell they were hitting the true notes, from her own responses as well as the open admiration of their fellow actors. Even from the cagey compliments of the enigmatic Bryce.

Oh, for heaven's sake, she implored her wayward mind, don't keep dredging up that man! As if she didn't have enough to contend with at the moment, her working arrangements with him seemed to have slumped into an uneasy truce, since that ridiculous altercation—and its even more ridiculous sequel, which she just couldn't quite manage to forget. Thank goodness, at least, Maria and Ben had been incorporated to take some of the strain off those heavy tutorials, no doubt at the request of John himself.

But no, she was concerned with finer preoccupations this evening. What were they? Ah, yes, she and Anthony. On stage they were definitely weaving the right spell, even though Anthony was only just memorising his lines. Even without benefit of costume or lighting or scenery, they were brewing the right chemistry. So where was she failing offstage? Her feelings for Anthony were so vividly enhanced by their enactment of Beatrice and Benedick's violent attraction. So how come *he* managed to be immune?

Or could he be guarding himself, aware that the torrent was bound to submerge them both in the end, but keeping his distance till it became inevitable? He was notorious for being doted on by many, but singling out none. Well, what of that? It was high time he took the plunge, and if Erinna wasn't the most eligible woman to take it with just now, who on earth was?

She knew, from the way his Benedick related to her Beatrice, that he was far from frigid. He could emanate a sensual glow, a vibrant humanity, which set her pulses racing—along with the pulses of most of the female on-lookers—exactly as it was designed to do. She refused to believe this was no more than stagecraft. He was a promising actor, but surely not a hypocrite? He had real, powerful feelings too, she could swear it.

She kept reminding herself they were hardly three weeks into rehearsals yet. Five or six weeks of term still to go, and excitement was bound to rise as the performance drew nearer. Anthony was bound to crack, eventually. Meanwhile, she must, she really must hang on to her dignity. Perhaps if she stopped inviting him, giving him hints—perhaps if she grew harder to get, he might grow more interested? After all, it worked like that with her, every time. Yes, that was her mistake: being too obvious. Anthony would enjoy the thrill of the chase, and she was depriving him of that male pleasure. Off-stage, she must hold back now, leave things to Shakespeare's brilliant magic.

She was half-way round the lake, and her tears dried as her determination hardened. Also, cold and exhaustion were percolating through the despair. She flagged, slowing to a walk, shoulders hunched. One last glance at the starlit lake and she turned off along the path which left the track and led back to the house-blocks.

That was when she became aware of this other set of footsteps, dogging hers. The other person had not stopped running when she did, so they were gaining fast. She panicked, conscious of her isolation in this dim, deserted spot. Then she reproached her over-fertile imagination. This enclosed campus was not normally a target for horrific attacks, or any of those ghastly things one was always hearing about in the media. Whoever they were, they had no less right than she did to be pounding round the lake after eleven at night.

All the same, she increased her speed as much as her faltering strength allowed, covering the ground at a low trot, head tucked well down...

'Erinna!'

She hesitated, then wheeled round. A man, calling her! Could it be Anthony? She deciphered the shape now emerging from the shadows. No, it couldn't. Bigger, darker.

'Erinna?'

Deeper voice, brisker. No, not Anthony. Dr John Bryce.

'Erinna, wait, for Christ's sake!'

She obeyed, eyeing him as he drew level.

'I had no idea you went in for midnight jogging, John. That's what I call taking fitness seriously. Or does it help you unwind after the exasperations of putting us through our petty paces?'

Panting slightly, he returned her stare. 'No, nocturnal jogging isn't really my thing. Once a day's my limit, preferably in the morning. Not bad training, though, when it comes to trying to catch up with Road-Runner Casey. What were you out to do, the three-minute mile?'

'Oh, I just felt like some air and exercise before turning in. Got to keep moving in this temperature, or you'd catch your death.' Erinna wrapped her arms around her body, seized by a shiver.

'Air and exercise?' His face was shadowed, but she could hear his scepticism. He laid a hand on her arm, propelling her onwards. 'Quite right, you should keep moving. Are you warm enough? Want to borrow my scarf?'

Meek from tiredness, she complied, but not without a sharp, sidelong glance. He sounded concerned, un-characteristically gentle, but his expression was unclear.

He was such a strange man, a mass of contradictions; like most men, when she came to think of it. A fairly weird lot, unpredictable, their outsides belying their in-sides. Why did she bother with them? she wondered, as she trudged wearily up the hill beside John Bryce.

'I'll be fine, thanks,' she said aloud. 'It's not far now.'

John grunted, keeping his stride in step with hers. After a few seconds, they both spoke at once.

'I expect you find rehearsals pretty draining?' John suggested.

'Did you say you were trying to catch up with me?' Erinna ventured.

They exchanged smiles, then Erinna continued. 'Yes, I do find them a bit shredding, but that's only because of all the work that goes into them. I'm sure you must get pretty wrung out, too? The amount of blood, sweat and tears you expend on us?'

'I enjoy it, or most of it, but I wondered, when you ran off like that tonight, whether you might be...' he cast a quick look round at her '...upset?'

Now she halted and swung to face him. 'How do you mean, upset?'

'I mean, upset. By anything that happened...'

'What sort of thing?'

'Anything that was said. By me, for instance. I can be a bit...harsh, I know.'

He stood at ease, studying her with a detached interest. Erinna felt threatened, and her hackles rose at once in defence.

'I can't think what gave you that idea! I was fine, just in need of—just wanted to get away on my own, let off some steam, that's all!'

He couldn't see her complexion, but he knew her cheeks would be fiery. 'A delicate mechanism, the artistic temperament,' he remarked.

She glared at him through the dimness. He had this confusing blend of tones, stern and benign; it was impossible to tell when he was mocking.

'You should know, Dr Bryce,' she muttered. Weariness fought irritation, and won. She gazed down, away from John's face and at their four feet, planted on the damp ground.

'You're making a fine job of Beatrice, you do know that, don't you?' There was a deliberate persistence about this inquisition, which Erinna was failing to understand.

'I'm very glad you think so,' she replied, cautiously pleased.

'And Anthony's not doing so badly, either.'

'I'm sure he'd be delighted to hear it. You must tell him.' She kept her tone steady, but she looked away as she said it.

'You generate some fair old sparks between you.'

'That's the general idea, isn't it?' Enough of this! Erinna turned from him and set off again. At this rate she wouldn't be able to stand up, let alone find cool replies to his peculiar questions and comments. What was his game, anyway, subjecting her to this...

His hand shot out and grabbed her shoulder, pulling her back so that she was forced to face him. 'Just one moment, Erinna. Don't run away.'

'I'm *not* running away!' She tried to shrug him off, but his grip only tightened. 'I'm tired, and cold, and I want...'

'I know. You want to escape to...'

'No, I *don't* want to escape!' she squeaked, infuriated now. 'I...'

'I was about to say, escape to a hot shower and a cosy bed. So do I. If we both walk on, we'll both get there all the sooner.'

She walked on; there seemed no choice. Especially as his hand stayed on her shoulder, his arm light but firm round her back. The sensation set up an instant tingling, yet it felt ludicrously right—in some odd way it fitted, so that Erinna lost the urge to evade it.

'Erinna, bear with me if I ask you something.'

She'd thought he had given up the cross-examination, but evidently he was only biding his time. She sighed. No doubt he was expecting her to fly off the handle, but she was far too tired, far too limp and harassed for fireworks tonight.

'Ask away,' she invited.

'About Anthony.'

'Oh, yes?' She was on guard again, despite her numbness. She knew John must feel her body stiffen, under his subtle, steering touch.

'I've been watching the way you and he get on.'

'I thought you said we were generating the right electricity?'

'Oh, yes, for Beatrice and Benedick. Excellent.' It seemed to Erinna that John was being unusually indirect. She wished he'd get to the point, whatever it was.

'So what's the problem?'

'There might not be a problem. That's what I'm trying to find out. I wouldn't want anything to spoil a beautiful relationship.'

Erinna was resolved not to boil over. She kept her steps very firm and even, to absorb some of the stress. 'Are we referring to the beautiful relationship between Beatrice and Benedick, or Anthony and me?'

'Both, in a way. Naturally my main concern is with the play.'

'What's wrong with the play? I'm not with you, John.'

He rallied his thoughts. His hand on her shoulder, his arm across her back, never faltered. 'I have this feeling you'd like to get closer to Anthony. The real Anthony, I mean. I'm sure you'll correct me if I'm wrong, but I do get the impression that you wish you could translate your stage affair into something more tangible—and that perhaps Anthony isn't...'

Now he did hesitate, no doubt searching for the most tactful phrase. Amazed at her own composure in the face of this blatant nerve, Erinna supplied a few for him. 'Isn't of like mind? Isn't so easily stirred by the genius of the Bard? Isn't so susceptible to the confusion of fantasy with reality?'

John was nodding, apparently relieved. So, he *had* expected her to jump off the deep end when he raised this tender topic. She couldn't blame him; she would have expected it herself, but something was teaching her a new circumspection—helping her to accept, rather than resent.

This exchange might be mildly agonising, but at least it gave her a chance to prove she could be as calm as the next person, as rational in her reactions, even when the next person happened to be John Bryce. And why should his opinion of her matter so much, in any case?

'I admire you for making it so easy for me, Erinna.'

He withdrew his arm from her shoulders, bringing her to a stop so that he could confront her. She felt the shrewdness of his gaze on her face.

'Think nothing of it.' She waved a breezy hand in his direction.

'So, am I right?' His tone had sharpened.

'What if you are? Would it be such a big deal? Would it threaten to undermine your production, if I felt that way about Anthony? Surely it would add an extra dimension to our stage romance?'

'It might—if your feelings were reciprocated.' John had become merciless now, reaching the nub of his message. 'But if they weren't, and you became disappointed—disillusioned—depressed—well, that might do a fair bit of harm. I've seen it happen before.'

'Let me get this straight.' Erinna spoke slowly, banking down a rising annoyance. 'You're warning me off Anthony because you're afraid my inclinations might ruin your precious play?'

'*Our* precious play,' John pointed out. 'Also, I wouldn't want you hurt, Erinna. I don't happen to think Anthony's very likely to...'

But Erinna's temper was billowing now, after its brief respite. 'How frightfully decent of you, not to want me hurt! I should be eternally grateful for your concern, for interesting yourself in my paltry affairs! But if you want to know, *Doctor* Bryce, I think it's a bloody insult! I think you don't have any notion what you're talking about! I think you should stick to your own business, and your books, and not stick your erudite nose in where it hasn't been invited.'

She waited to see if he would pick up the gauntlet, but he simply stood, silent and solemn, so she carried on with her tirade.

'As for what I feel, or what Anthony Travers feels, I ought to have pointed out to you several minutes ago that it has nothing whatsoever to do with you, but for some crazy reason, I didn't. Whatever's going on between us, or not going on, you have my promise that it won't affect my rendition of Beatrice. I shall make sure it doesn't. Satisfied?'

Her voice had climbed to a peak and dropped again. Now she ended on a comparatively controlled note. This wasn't destined to be one of her really spectacular eruptions. Given the aggravation, it should have been, but sheer weariness had tempered it.

Now, before emotion could overcome her again, she stepped back from John, making to leave him without another word.

Once again he was too quick for her, reaching out to pull her back.

'I'm truly sorry, Erinna.' He sounded utterly sincere, even humble, so that she felt more confused than ever. 'I meant to warn you, offer a friendly word of advice— as your director—or support. I'm not sure...'

He was drawing her nearer. She did not resist. The righteous indignation still seethed, but it seemed to be converging with other feelings: anger, mingled with anxiety, uncertainty, frustration, and a new floodtide of passion which bore the rest along and obliterated them.

But how could this be happening? This man had just enraged her, mortified her and embarrassed her. Not only that, he was the wrong man; he was not Anthony!

She waited in a kind of trance, knowing he was going to kiss her again. But he did not. He held her face in both his hands, cupping her cheeks, thumbs under her chin; exploring her, earnestly, deeply, with his eyes. Right on cue, the moon emerged from behind some trees to floodlight the lake and silver-plate John and Erinna into a pale tableau, an old, arty photograph in black and white.

When his eyes had drunk their fill, his mouth did take over, with extreme tenderness—the lightest of flutters, brushing her brow, eyelids, nose, cheeks, chin and, finally, with exquisite subtlety, her lips. The most restrained, lingering taste, and just as she melted, opening her mouth to his, he was gone. His face had lifted from hers, to bury itself among the richness of her hair, cold in the cold air, yet warmly soft against her skin.

He stayed motionless, his arms about her. Erinna stood equally transfixed, shutting out all thought, aware only of that warm, close contact. Demanding nothing, so that she yearned to give everything. Comforting, yet unbearably tantalising. Tearing her between alarm and desire, the ultimate female conflict, and she was experiencing it, for the first time, here in the unlikely haven of John Bryce's arms!

After a churning minute, alarm gained the upper hand. Erinna fought free and took two paces back, out of temptation, out of danger. John let her go, his expression impassive, body still as stone in the moonglow.

'I really have to go now.'

She was mumbling, adding a few more words to that effect, including garbled phrases like 'much too late', and 'nearly there', as she waved a vague hand at her hall of residence, now looming some fifty yards ahead. John watched and listened intently, but he said nothing.

Then she fled, stumbling once as she crossed the uneven ground, finding a final fragile spurt of energy for the short home stretch.

John went on watching until she had safely entered the building. Then he swung on his heel and made off in another direction.

CHAPTER SIX

TONIGHT had to be the night. When would it ever happen, if not at the Valentine's Ball?

If Anthony was ever going to get the message, surely it must be here, under these rainbow strobe-lights? Gyrating to the insistent disco pulse of this top live band, specially hired by the Students' Union for the occasion, at crippling expense? With Erinna wearing her gorgeous jade silk—figure-hugging, shimmering—picked up for a song in one of those trendy shops, featuring authentic gear from the Thirties and Forties, during a recent visit to the city.

She was spectacular and she knew it, with the creamy curves of shoulders and throat rising from the daring scooped neckline; her hair up in carelessly soft sophistication, kindly arranged by Lisa; her make-up bolder than usual, to match the spirit of the dress—a generous shading of green about the eyes, a richer red on the lips, leaving the cheeks translucently pale by contrast.

There was no shortage of would-be partners. Faithful Mike headed the queue, followed by plenty of others just as eager, making no secret of their stunned admiration. Erinna bopped and laughed, drank and socialised. But her gaze constantly strayed to where Anthony held court, sharing drinks and jokes, always smooth and popular.

He looked fantastic in the black tuxedo and frilled shirt: groomed, perfectly presented. It sent darts of pleasure through Erinna, just to see him. After she'd finished this Dubonnet and lemon, and this chat with

Clare and Tariq—no, she'd promised Tariq a dance, too, so it would have to be after that—she was going to make her way over there, subtly incorporate herself into Anthony's group, and pluck up the courage to ask him for a dance. After all, it was only fitting that Beatrice should take to the floor with Benedick, once or twice at least. Especially at a Valentine's Ball. And just now, when she had cast yet another surreptitious look in Anthony's direction, she was sure she'd caught him out, casting an equally quick but intense look at her.

Tariq was an expert traditional dancer, rare among her crowd, and she was rather enjoying this slower number, lightly held in his arms. No complications, no pressure; just the music, the movement, the relaxing company of a good friend who never needed nor wanted to be more than that...

'Excuse me.'

Tariq swept them to a halt and stood back with a nod and a smile. Erinna confronted the intruder, wide-eyed.

'I believe this *is* a Gentlemen's Excuse-Me?'

Anthony had beaten her to it! Here he was, not just requesting her favours, but positively hijacking them! Erinna's heart soared, but she kept her joy well concealed—the start of her new campaign.

'Was it? I didn't realise!' She turned to Tariq.

'Oh, yes, it was. They announced it when you were in the cloakroom, just before they began playing.' Tariq was quite happy to hand her over to the other man.

'Well, if you don't mind, Tariq...'

'Of course not! Why should I?'

'He's in no position to mind,' Anthony pointed out, but his tone and smile were loaded with charm. 'I'm a gentleman, and this is our excuse-me, so excuse us, Tariq, or there won't be any of it left.'

Then he was leading Erinna off on to the dance-floor. His hands were exactly right, as she knew they would be, on her waist and at her back: neither too firm nor too flimsy, guiding and clasping with just that touch of possessive intimacy which all women appreciated, without being swamped or smothered. He had a supple body and he moved it superbly, but then she knew that, from witnessing Benedick in action.

It was hypnotic rather than exhilarating, fitting herself to him, swaying in time with him and the rhythm of the music. There was none of that painful excitement, that dark thrill which springs from danger, or shock, or resentment, or confusion—some paradoxical surge of mixed responses. But who needed that feeling? Not Erinna, certainly! She'd been learning more than enough about its threats and hassles lately, and she could do without them.

No, this was different; she knew where she was with this. It felt wonderful but manageable, romantic but safe, just the way it ought to feel. Erinna floated high on a cloud nine of pride, knowing what a fine couple they must make—so blond and so auburn, moving in unison.

Thank goodness no other gentleman butted in for his turn, but the number had to end eventually, and she braced herself for the inevitable separation. Anthony held her for those vital seconds longer than necessary, before releasing her to smile into her face. Erinna knew this was only the beginning. Here it came at last, the realisation of all those hopes and dreams; the fantasy made flesh...

'I thank you for that, Beatrice!' He made a dashing Elizabethan bow.

'The honour was mine, Benedick.' Her deep curtsy was demurely flirtatious.

'Maybe there'll be a Ladies' Excuse-Me later.'
Anthony's smile was as charming as ever, but perhaps
a little fixed.

'Pardon? Oh, I see. Yes, I expect there will.'

'I'm going out for a breath of air now, but we must
have another dance before the evening's over.' Shooting
his immaculate cuff, he glanced at his watch. 'You look
stunning, did I tell you? The belle of the ball, no
question. Cheers, Erinna!'

Before she could reply, he was turning away with a
jaunty wave and setting off to where he had left his
Dramsoc cronies, propping up a bar at the far end of
the hall. Erinna could only stand and stare, as that
beautiful, confident figure receded. Her delight evaporated in a steam of puzzled disappointment.

It was her fault, for being so complacent—one
skirmish and she allowed herself to think the war was
won! Clearly, more effort was going to be needed yet,
on her part, but if Anthony reckoned she was hanging
about, coyly waiting for a Ladies' Excuse-Me, he had
another think coming. He was keen on her, surely, and
anyone could see they made a great pair, on the dance-
floor as well as on stage. Now, he was off out for a
breath of air, he'd told her so—wasn't that as good as
a direct invitation? The next move was up to her. He'd
thrown the ball into her court, and here she was, ready
and willing to catch it.

She'd downed a few drinks, unusual for her. A drop
of Dutch courage never did any harm at a moment of
challenge. Without pausing to risk changing her mind,
she marched through the throng in the direction he had
taken.

Some of his friends still sat at the bar, but he was not
among them. Probably outside by now, relishing a
peaceful cigarette. Instinct led her through a side door

nearby. It wasn't a bad night: cloudy, not particularly clear or atmospheric. Rather a shame, everyone had moaned, for a Valentine's Ball—but not freezing, at least. Now, where would he wait, hoping Erinna would seek him out, preparing for the next chapter in their budding love story?

A few couples strolled hand in hand, or leaned against walls, lost in their private worlds. Erinna followed the path round the side of the building to a narrow clump of trees, well off the beaten track and out of sight of passers-by. Just the sort of spot anyone might choose if they wanted to be alone, or undiscovered by all except that one special person.

Someone else had got here first, and he or she certainly wasn't alone. They were very much part of a pair, standing under one of the trees, close together. Erinna could barely make out the two forms, intertwined among the shadows. She sensed, rather than saw, heartfelt passion when she met it, and now she turned tactfully away, leaving them to their mutual discovery.

She carried on past them along the same path, towards the back of the hall, where it was just as quiet, with grassy slopes and bushes. She was sure Anthony would have headed that way. Before she was out of earshot, she became aware that the couple under the tree were conversing in low voices.

Low voices, but distinct. And one of them, at least, was surely familiar? Erinna paused to shoot a curious glance over her shoulder. The two figures now leaned against a tree trunk, no longer touching, but still exuding that air of heated intimacy which can mean only one relationship.

It was none of Erinna's business, but she found herself transfixed by the pair, by something about them—something indefinable... And at that precise moment, as she looked, a half-moon emerged from behind a ragged cloud mass, shedding light on the little tableau, and into certain unlit corners of Erinna's mind.

No wonder the couple had arrested her attention! They might seem superficially conventional, but in fact they were strangely incompatible. The woman was petite, informal, with short, dark, curly hair. In those tight denim jeans and the chunky sweater, she clearly had not been at the Ball. Smoke from her cigarette curled upwards into the night, as she addressed her partner in urgent, fluent tones.

Erinna recognised her—unmistakable in voice, stance, image. She was mad on theatre, and often helped with costumes, scenery and props in productions for the Drama Department. Erinna admired her energy and vitality, sensing a kindred spirit—a woman dedicated to the honesty of instinct and emotion—even though she had exchanged very few words with her. She was thirty if she was a day, and surely she was married to that rather pompous senior lecturer in the Applied Electronics field, or some such dreary technological subject?

As for the young man—certainly no older than Erinna—he wore a dinner-jacket and white shirt. He was tall and extremely fair, so that he gleamed silver-white under the moon's rays, shining head bent close to the woman's dark one as he listened intently to her every syllable. Only one person had hair like that, gestured like that, leaned like that, spoke like that...

Yes, Anthony Travers' educated drawl wafted across to Erinna now. He was speaking quite softly, but the sound reached her ears as loud and clear as if he had been inches away. There was no mistaking it, or him, but he was animated in a new way. She had never seen him like this, suffused with a warmth which he rarely permitted himself to display in public, especially offstage.

Even from this distance, and in the clutches of pure shock, Erinna did not doubt that she was witnessing the real, uncensored Anthony—and for the first time. She was being presented with fact, stark fact, incontrovertible, staring her in the face. Obvious, with the benefit of hindsight—but how foolish it made her feel, unsuspecting for so long! Now it rang all the more true, for being so carefully concealed and guarded.

It was a cruel way to stumble on such a revelation. Its significance went so much deeper than just being about Anthony himself; she was faced with some painful working-out on her own account, too. Returning to the Ball would be a pointless waste of time. She must be locked away, alone, if she was to absorb the implications of this bombshell.

They hadn't seen her, they were far too engrossed in each other. Heart pounding, trying to control the shudder which was already creeping over her body, Erinna took off as fast as her glamorous spiky heels would allow—away from the scene, away from the Union, towards the seclusion of her own room.

John Bryce's dashboard clock told him it was nineteen minutes past midnight. Another Saturday gone, another two-hundred-mile motorway sprint safely accomplished.

Not that he didn't enjoy his weekend expeditions; they were pleasure, as well as duty. But this week he was more frayed than usual, with one consideration and another, plus the fact that he was shaking off a heavy head cold. Altogether it was a relief to be pulling in through the campus gates at the crack of Sunday, rather than Monday as it often was.

The place had not exactly packed up for the night. Plenty of lights and action still in evidence, with festive sounds floating over from the Union. It wasn't late by student standards, of course, especially for a Saturday, and there was bound to be some function on. Some excuse to bop and booze the small hours away—if they needed one, which John doubted.

He shook his head, but he was smiling. He'd mingled with students across the world, and this lot were a reasonable bunch on the whole. He kept himself aloof, but he appreciated their company—all that untarnished, youthful enthusiasm—more than they guessed. It had been a sticky inner struggle for John, deciding to accept the Dramsoc's invitation to direct *Much Ado*, but he was glad he'd taken the plunge. With a bit of luck, and a lot of self-discipline, its rewards would surely outweigh its complexities—in the end.

Passing the Union, he slowed down to avoid jaywalkers, an assortment of them in groups and pairs, lurching perilously along the roadside. Whatever this occasion, it merited the full fancy regalia: suits and ties, old-fashioned ballgowns. The revellers waved happily at him and grinned through his car windows. Whoever he was, he was welcome to join in their celebrations.

John waved back, then stifled a yawn as he left them behind. He must focus his concentration for this darker stretch of road which led to the student house-blocks, then continued to the far edge of the campus, where staff were accommodated. Round this corner, twenty yards from the only undergraduate Hall he had ever actually visited, that unfortunate evening he was doing his best to censor out, when...

'Bloody hell!'

The figure was tottering along, right on the brow of the road. John was forced to swerve violently to avoid hitting it. At the same time, it scooted nimbly aside and hopped up on the grass verge; a bit late to take evasive action now, he snarled to himself, as his front wheels crunched on the kerb.

His engine stalled and he cursed roundly. The figure apparently hesitated, decided not to abandon the scene of the crime, and made its way back to the car.

Definitely female, shapely, in a slinky, silky dress, now vividly spotlit in John's headlamps. Somewhat the worse for wear, by the look of her, but with a stubborn air about the way she headed towards him. As if life had dealt her a few blows already, and this one wasn't about to knock her in a heap.

He wound his window down. 'What the blazes are you doing in the middle of the road?' he barked.

'There's hardly anyone driving about at this time of night,' she retorted, 'and anyway, weren't you going a bit fast for...'

'Erinna!'

Her hair was free of its moorings, her make-up smudged and she was shivering pathetically. John was sure he could see tear stains on her cheeks.

'Oh no, it's you,' she said, unflatteringly.

'What's the matter? What's happened? What are you doing here?'

'Shall I answer them all at once, or one at a time?' Her speech might be slightly slurred, her voice choked, but her native wit was intact.

John responded by reaching across to fling his offside door open and hauling her in beside him before she could register, let alone protest. He switched on the interior light and inspected her with great thoroughness, from face to feet. She sat with her hands primly folded, uncomplaining, almost catatonic, staring glassily ahead. Her expression suggested this was all part of some extended nightmare, and, if she held herself rigid, it might just go away—and John with it.

When he had finished assessing her, he gazed out into the night for a few seconds, frowning as he drummed his fingers on the steering wheel. Then, as if jumping to an instant irrevocable decision, he turned the key in the ignition, charging the engine into life. At once he reversed away from the kerb and shot off down the road, past Erinna's Hall, and some playing fields, and another Hall, and still on...

The reality of all this was seeping through to Erinna. Where she was, and above all, who she was with. Now she was trembling, from inner stress as much as outer cold, hugging her unprotected body with bare arms.

'Where are we g-going?'

'To sort you out. Whatever you've been up to, you're in a proper old mess. You need a hot, strong drink and a thick pullover. And that's before we even *ask* what the hell you've been playing at, to get into this state! Or why you're braving the elements with nothing on but that scrap of silk. Highly ornamental it may be, but I'd hardly call it practical, in these conditions.'

'I left my coat in the Union cloakroom.' Erinna's explanation was so subdued, even humble, she was surprised at herself. It ought to feel threatening, infuriating, being organised by him like this. Strangely, it felt logical, even welcome. In line with accepting the insults he threw at her on stage, or his more caustic comments at the end of her essays...or not wanting to struggle, when his arm came round her or his lips claimed hers, however hard she tried to avoid recalling those moments, or facing up to them...

'You and coats seem to have a doomed relationship.'

She forced a wan smile, as he parked efficiently outside the small, select block, designed for the convenience of single senior staff. Then he locked the car doors and bundled her quickly into his flat. It was simple but adequate, with living-room, bedroom, kitchen and bathroom. Furnished basically, rather than luxuriously—but so blessedly warm! The central heating was still cosily turned up, and it was the only greeting Erinna cared about at this minute.

The promised thick pullover was in a rich chocolate brown, worn to a pleasing mellowness, softly handknitted. On Erinna it was voluminous, of course, its sleeves hanging three inches over her hands, its hemline reaching to mid-thigh.

Snugly cocooned in its folds, while John disappeared to the kitchen, she curled up in a corner of John's sofa, closing her eyes, surrendering to silence and seclusion.

The sweater smelled of soapflakes, laced with a tantalising seasoning of Bryce. What did it consist of, a man's particular scent? His own brand of aftershave, soap or talc; the detergent he used to wash his clothes; whether he smoked or not—in John's case, not; and other, less tangible ingredients, to do with skin and body chemistry and...

'You OK in there?' he called.

'Fine.' It was all so soporific, she could barely raise her voice to reply.

He came through, carrying two hefty ceramic mugs, and set them down on the low table. Then he joined her, at the opposite end of the sofa. She noticed subliminally how tired he looked: brow furrowed, eyelids heavy, mouth tight.

'Had a tough weekend?' she wondered, sympathetic.

'No tougher than usual, and shorter than some.' He seemed put out, perhaps by finding the tables turned, when he had expected to do the interrogating.

'Been far?' She nursed the mug in both hands, absorbing the heat through her pores, inhaling the steam.

'Round trip of about four hundred miles.' The way he said it, you might have thought it was just down the road and he did it every day.

Actually, she remembered, he did it every week. Whatever it was. A coil of curiosity began to twitch and unwind. 'Anywhere special?'

He flashed her an indirect, lop-sided grin, which said, if you're going to be nosey, I'm going to be cagey. 'Depends what you mean by special,' he said lazily. 'It's something I'm well used to doing. Something I do regularly. A strong personal commitment, you might say.'

If ever information had been uninformative, this was it. Erinna took a diversionary sip from her mug, while she assimilated it.

'How did you know I'd rather have tea than coffee? And how did you know I take milk but no sugar?'

John shrugged. 'Sixth sense? Instinctive hospitality?' He took a swig himself. 'Or maybe it's just that I much prefer tea, and I don't take sugar, and you're on my patch so you take what I give you.'

'Ah.' She sipped some more and felt her mind and body relax as she gazed round the room. 'Quite a decent place they give you. I've never been in here before. Lowly undergraduates are rarely invited into these exalted regions. In fact...' she cast him a glance '...I always understood it's not encouraged.'

'It's against regulations,' he told her calmly. 'Except at officially approved social events. With a minimum of two guests at a time. Preferably of the same gender as the host.'

'So how come you're prepared to stick your professional head on the block, for my sake?' she demanded. 'Not to mention possibly putting *my* insignificant career at risk? Are you just one of nature's anarchists?'

John studied her, and suddenly she wished she was less dishevelled, smeared and generally battered. She should have had a wash in his bathroom before making herself at home in his living-room, but it was too late now; he was registering every sordid detail, and there was nothing she could do but meet his gaze.

'I can give you three answers to that one.' He counted them off on his fingers. 'First, no one's likely to notice or find out, at one o'clock in the morning, as long as they don't happen to see you arrive or leave. Second, I'm quite sure exceptions may be made in emergencies. Rules are there to be broken, after all. And third, we're both leaving this establishment in a few months' time, so it wouldn't really be worth anyone kicking up a fuss even if they did find out. Does that make you feel any better?'

Erinna stretched. 'I wasn't feeling especially bad. I just thought you might be, as a member of the Faculty...'

'A visiting member only. I came on a temporary contract. I'm only here till June, same as you.'

'I thought you came for two years, not one?'

'I did, but I've just been offered a plum post in the States, starting next October, so I'm sliding out of my second year here.'

'I see.' Erinna digested this. 'Joining the Brain Drain? Don't the University authorities take rather a dim view?'

'I've been part of the Brain Drain for years,' he reminded her. 'This will be more like going home, for me, than going abroad. I've spent more than half my working life in America and Canada. As for the authorities here, no, they don't mind that much. My contract was open-ended anyway, and it's a real peach of a professorship over there—quite a bit of second-hand kudos for them, in a way. So everyone's quite happy.'

Erinna was deep in thought. 'You're kind of—on the fringes, aren't you, John? A citizen of the world—peripatetic—fancy-free? You never really have been part of this little community, have you?'

'I wouldn't describe myself as fancy-free, exactly.' John was frowning, as if she had touched a raw nerve. 'As I've just told you, I do have certain major commitments that are nothing to do with my academic life, but no less important to me. Probably more important.'

'You mean personal, rather than professional?' Erinna kept her tone light, but the coil of curiosity unravelled a bit further. Would these personal commitments have a feminine face, by any chance? And maybe feminine hands, which had lovingly knitted this voluptuous garment she was now swathed in?

'I suppose you could describe it that way.' His message was clear: she'd probed as deep as he could afford to let her.

'I see,' she said again. It was far from true: she didn't see at all, and she wished she did. But it was time to shift the subject, and he seemed to have retreated inside his head so she'd have to take the initiative. 'Did you say something about emergencies? Does this constitute one, in your opinion?'

John was quick to follow her lead, away from his affairs and back to hers. 'That depends on what was going on. It looked pretty dramatic when I nearly demolished you on the road. But appearances can be deceptive. You seem to have made a remarkable recovery.'

'I do feel better, actually,' she admitted. 'Thanks to the tea and...'

'Sympathy? You haven't given me a chance to offer much of that yet!'

'And the extra layer of clothing, I was going to say.'

After a brief pause, during which they gazed in opposite directions, John turned abruptly to her. 'Do you want to tell me what was wrong? You don't have to, of course.'

'No, I don't have to.' Erinna was defensive, but there was a sincere concern in John's eyes, and no pressure. On the spur of the moment, she made up her mind to tell him anyway. Where was the harm? It might make her feel less stupid, confessing to someone; and John was involved, in a way, whether she liked it or not. Also, she had this peculiar sensation that he knew already; part of the general feeling he gave her, as if he was inside her head—more in tune with her, at some obscure level, than she was herself.

'That's all right,' he was saying, but she interrupted, drawing her knees comfortably up underneath her for moral support.

'It's the Valentine's Ball, as you no doubt realise.'

'Valentine's! Of course, that's the...'

'Right. St Valentine. You know, hearts and flowers, moonlight and roses. Dare I say it, Dr Bryce—romance? Too juvenile and sentimental for your austere tastes.'

As she said it, she felt less than enraptured about the whole thing, herself. Disillusioned, embittered, distinctly unromantic.

'If you say so, Erinna.' He was watching her closely, keeping the focus on her, giving nothing away.

'I was having a good time. Nothing special, a few drinks—not that I can afford many—a few dances...'

'No one special?' John prompted, as she faltered.

She was taken off guard. 'I didn't have you down as a matchmaker! The bow and arrow might suit you quite well, but the dinky little wings and...'

'I'm not prying. I told you, you don't have to tell me any of this.' After a moment's thought, he added, 'And more of the Sir Galahad than the Cupid, if you don't mind. I think I'll file this one under "Rescue of Distressed Damsel", even if I never get to find out what the distress was about.'

Erinna found it surprisingly easy to smile, then continue with her tale, which grew more ridiculous in the telling. Her tone developed an edge of satire, aimed entirely at herself.

'I wanted one thing tonight, more than anything in the world.' She looked John in the eye, without false modesty or embarrassment. 'Or rather, one person.'

'Would this have anything to do with our friend Benedick?'

'You don't miss a lot, from your director's chair, do you?'

'I recognise real emotion when I see it.'

'And you saw it when you looked at me looking at Anthony?' He nodded, and Erinna nodded back, ruefully. God, how transparent she must have been! 'So, you won't be amazed to learn how thrilled I was when Anthony asked me to dance. He's a lovely dancer.'

'I can imagine.' John nodded again, perfectly serious.

'You know, don't you?' Suddenly Erinna rounded on him, her voice and her poise cracking at last. 'I expect everyone in the whole of Dramsoc—everyone on the whole *campus*—knew, except Muggins here!'

'Know?' John was supremely discreet.

'That Anthony's having a—an affair, or something, with—what's her name? Lindsay, isn't it? That...'

'The charming wife of my erudite colleague, Dr Leonard Baxter.' John was nodding, apparently unperturbed. 'I had my suspicions, but you're wrong on one point, Erinna. I'm willing to bet very few others realise it, not even Anthony's own friends. He's not the guy to broadcast such a thing around. But one does develop a nose for these vibes between...'

'*You* might. I didn't! Not until I stumbled across them tonight, minutes after dancing with him! They must have had some kind of a tryst, and there I was, misunderstanding his messages, following him out there, expecting...' She covered her face with her hands, scarlet from deferred shame at the time she had wasted, the potential ridicule she had brought on herself. Then she uncovered her face and stared at John, as an even more painful truth hit her. 'You tried to warn me about this, the other night, didn't you?'

'I tried. But you weren't too receptive.' His words might be bleak, but the tone was gentle.

'No. I wasn't, was I?' Erinna bit her lip. 'I didn't want to hear. Whatever you were trying to say about him, I knew I wouldn't like it.'

'Don't blame yourself.' John was still gentle. It was surprising, more disconcerting than the reproach which she knew she deserved. 'How could you have known? He seems so available; in fact he makes a point of just that. Isn't it all part of the game, the deception? Actually, I suspect they may be pretty serious about each other,' he added, his voice hardening. 'Otherwise they wouldn't bother to be quite so scrupulous about not being seen—not flouting the rules, all that stuff...'

'But I should have *guessed*!' Erinna groaned. 'I feel such a fool! The way he behaved, and he never has any real girlfriends...'

'It wasn't just the other night.' Now things were opening out, John seemed determined to follow them through. 'I had it in the back of my mind right from the start, when you first asked me to take the play on. Remember, you told me he was going to be Benedick to your Beatrice, and there was something about the way you looked...'

'I remember.' Erinna cringed. That evening, in her room! Was she likely to forget, however hard she tried? 'Fantasy and reality! You delivered your stock lecture, or at least, that's how it seemed then.' Her sigh came up from her bare toes. 'You weren't so far wrong about me, after all, John. In the tutorial, or out of it. I *do* live in a dream world. I *am* too busy craving the impossible to notice hard fact under my nose. My friend Lisa was right, too. I always go for men who could never go for me. It's as if I...as if I don't even really *want* them to!'

With this self-discovery, her voice wavered, and tears crept from the corners of each eye. She scrabbled helplessly for her evening bag.

'Have mine.' John was handing her a large, folded handkerchief. 'It's clean.'

'Wouldn't care if it wasn't,' she mumbled, accepting it gratefully and scrubbing furiously at her face. It was never going to be the same again, wiping off all this lipstick and mascara, but she'd buy him a replacement. 'Bloody men!' she erupted, after a good loud blow of her nose. 'Why do they have to make life so complicated?'

'They?' John's smile was mildly ironic.

'Sorry. I'm not forgetting you're one as well. It's just...' She took refuge in burying her face in the hanky again.

'I understand, I think.'

She glanced at him, alerted through her misery. Surely he was above feeling offended or threatened if she excluded him from her outburst against the rest of his sex? Essentially male, grimly rational he might be, but she didn't see him as spuriously macho or insecure.

No, he was smiling broadly. He meant it when he said he understood. Unlike many men—perhaps most men—he was innately sensitive.

'I'm sorry about all this, John.' She twisted the handkerchief between her fingers. 'I don't know why I'm here, or telling you this...'

'You're here because I nearly flattened you under my front tyres. You're telling me because I asked you, maybe because you need to.' He leaned closer. 'Now you've found out the truth, and you're already getting used to the idea. In a few weeks, or even days, you'll have got over it and be back to normal.'

She eyed him doubtfully. 'You're being very sweet.'

'So, there's another discovery to add to tonight's score.'

'Appearances are deceptive?'

'Something like that,' he agreed, gravely.

'Will this affect our—my performance in the play, do you think?'

'That's entirely up to you, Erinna. I don't see why it should. I realised the sparks you struck off each other weren't all theatrical—not from your point of view, at least—but I have faith in your self-discipline and your pride. I'll lay any odds no one's going to guess a thing.'

'Not even Anthony?'

'Not if you play your cards right.'

'I hope I can. I'm enjoying this play so much—I mean, altogether, apart from all this...' Her tears had stopped now, but she blushed. 'In a funny way, it's a relief to know the truth. I think I was finding it more frustrating than rewarding.'

'Hardly surprising.' John's smile was wry. 'I'm glad you're enjoying the play. You're a marvellous Beatrice, however much I may rant at you. I only ever rant at people who——' his tone hardened, and he turned away '—who show promise.'

Yes, she showed promise: as an actress, a Shakespearian interpreter, a star student, a probable first-class degree. No wonder he took such a kind interest in her welfare! It impinged quite a bit on his own.

'You're working wonders. We're all really impressed.' She made herself sound as gracious and grateful as she could. It wasn't easy, but she succeeded.

John was stretching himself out, leaving one arm lying along the back of the sofa so that it just reached her shoulder. 'Some mutual admiration society this is turning out to be! More tea?'

'Oh, no, thanks. It must be incredibly late. I ought to go.'

'Is it safe to let you out alone? No more suicidal plunges under passing cars?'

'I feel quite all right now, thanks.' She made to get up.

Without shifting an inch, he restrained her with the hand on her shoulder. She sat down again, wondering what was coming next. And wondering even more why she hoped it was something so totally personal and intimate. She should be making a headlong dash for escape from it, rather than sitting here, willing it to happen.

'Before you go, Erinna...'

'Yes?' Her eyes were wide, full of conflicting fears and desires.

'One last question of a personal nature—since we've been into psychology here, and I happen to be interested in the human condition.'

'What?' The apprehension turned to suspicion.

'Do you have any idea *why* you're like this about men? Preferring the safe fantasy to the dangerous flesh?'

'It's not that I reject the flesh,' she protested impetuously.

'So I've noticed.' He grinned, and her blush deepened. 'That's one of the things that make you so intriguing. Such an exotic mixture of pure sensuality with sensual purity. The original passionate virgin.'

She met his challenge with honesty. There was no point in denying what must be patently obvious, clear as daylight to this no doubt experienced man of the world. 'So what did you mean—*why?*'

'I meant, what's made you like this? Rejecting the reality of men in your life, keeping them at a secure distance? Locking them in your dreams, rather than your arms? What's made you so defensive, Erinna?' He moved up towards her, so that his hand slid along her neck to lie on the other shoulder. His body touched hers, all the way down, side pressed to side—reassuring, yet stimulating. 'What are you so afraid of?' he murmured.

'I'm not afraid, exactly. It's more...'

'More what?' But his pressure was so quiet, so careful.

'More anger than fear. You're right, John. It goes back to—to when I was very young. It's a psychologist's dream. It was my father, you see...' She shut her eyes, and clenched her fists. She never, ever talked about this, but she wasn't giving up now. It was as if John had given her the chance to unburden herself—but to herself, rather than to him.

He nodded, with wise simplicity. 'It often is.'

'I was ten, the oldest in the family. I've got five brothers and sisters, and at that time they ranged from two to eight. Molly and Bridie are twins,' she explained, as John's eyebrows arched. 'They must be—let me see—eighteen now...'

He whistled. 'Six is a fair tally, with or without twins!'

'We're Irish, in case it had escaped your notice. Catholic, you see.'

'All the same! So, what happened in this trauma at ten years old?''

'Nothing very outlandish or bizarre. My father walked out on us. That's all.'

'That's all?' His hold on her tightened. 'That's enough.'

He was so encouraging, it made her task a bit less impossible. At this moment, she could think of no one else in the world she could even begin to tell this to. Not the full gruesome facts of it; not even her friends, who knew only the barest outline.

'He just disappeared. With the wife of one of his colleagues, or so we always understood. Mother doesn't say a lot about it.' Erinna didn't bother to disguise her bitterness. 'We've never heard from him or set eyes on him since that day. He was a clerk in a Government department. I was born in Tipperary, but we moved into Dublin when I was a baby. My mother was distraught, of course, when it happened... I'll never forget...'

'Poor woman! And you poor kid! I bet you carried some of the responsibility—and a load of guilt?' he added, half to himself.

'She was left almost penniless, with no income and six kids.'

'How the hell did she manage?' John seemed utterly involved in the situation, as if the people were real and known to him, and it was happening now instead of years ago. That was what made him so unusual, because to Erinna this was how it always *did* seem. To her, it was still happening. In her heart, it went on happening every day.

'She got by. It wasn't easy,' she told him. 'She was a trained nursery teacher. We came to England, where jobs were easier to come by. She wanted to make a new life, I think. She's worked full-time ever since. I've only ever been across the water on holiday. I'd love to go back—in one way, but in another...'

'You never want to set foot in the place again?'

She glanced at him. 'That's right. Anyway, I left school at sixteen and went straight out to work in a shop, to help out. But after a couple of years, Mum persuaded me to go back to college and take my A-levels. I'd always wanted to go to University, and she wanted me to, but I felt I ought to...'

'To contribute to the family coffers?'

'They're never full enough with all those growing mouths to feed,' Erinna said sadly. 'I should never really have come, but she insisted.'

'She sounds like a fine woman. Has she never re-married, then?'

'No way. She's had offers, but she says she's had enough of men. She's devoted herself to us, especially the little ones, who never really knew our father...'

Erinna could only just bring herself to mention him, without choking on years of accumulated rage and disgust.

'You've never forgiven him, have you, Erinna?'

Erinna shook her head. 'My mother says she has, but I can't.'

'We're not all tarred with the same brush, you know.' John's voice was as warm and close as his body. 'But I can understand how, and why...I can see how you came to be the way you are.' He paused, then added on a lighter note, 'I also see why you're somewhat older than most of your fellow Finalists. Somewhat more mature, too.'

'*More* mature?' After everything he knew about her, he could say that?

'There are ways and ways of being mature, Erinna. Some of them are more important than others. All of them can be learned.'

'I suppose so.' But she wasn't convinced... and now these conflicts, the ancient pain of these revelations, combined with the heavy sense of his arm around her, were all becoming stifling... overwhelming...

'I think it's really time I went now, John,' she muttered. 'I think it's time I...' She was washed out, spent, and so drowsy. Her head slumped sideways against his shoulder.

'Poor little Erinna.' Did he mean here and now, or the bereft ten-year-old child he had just glimpsed, staunchly fighting the male world on behalf of her beloved mother? Did it matter which he meant?

His face and voice hazed as he drew his arm slowly away, and she slipped down among the cushions.

'I think it's...' she tried one last time, before sinking under.

'And I think,' John said quietly, as he went to find a spare duvet and tuck it carefully round her, 'it's time you had a long, peaceful sleep, Miss Casey.'

CHAPTER SEVEN

ERINNA half opened her eyes, but they snapped shut again, as if weighted with lead. This dull ache throbbed behind them. This uneasiness, which penetrated through to her brain, her mind. This knowledge that all was not as it should be.

She was scrunched up in an awkward position on an unfamiliar bed. Or was it a bed? It felt even smaller than the one in her room, and a different shape. Her body was jammed against a backrest with soft cushions, not the usual wall. She was snugly covered with a quilt, not the usual sheet and blankets. And she was wearing something positively outlandish, not her usual pyjamas.

She prised her eyelids up again and peered round the room. There were plain linen curtains, drawn together, but that was certainly daylight on the outside of them. And more than enough of it filtering inside for Erinna to see and remember where she was, and why.

She sat bolt upright, pushing aside the duvet. Immediately, her head reeled, her stomach churned, and she wished she hadn't. A lot more alcohol must have been involved last night than her system was used to. On top of that, the heightened emotion, the release of pent-up confidences...no wonder she felt done over this morning, as if she'd been turned inside-out and given a thorough shaking.

Thorough, but remarkably gentle. John's motives for all that personal probing were obscure, but he'd set about it in such a calmly direct way, Erinna suspected he knew just what he was after. She only wished *she* did. She might not be a mystery to him any more, but he was increasingly puzzling to her.

Come to that, she was fairly puzzling to herself, too. The amount she still had to understand about herself, her own fancies and foibles, seemed to swell every day. In fact it was daunting, the prospect of embarking on this voyage of discovery, with or without the steady Bryce hand at the helm, as it had clearly been last night.

She stood up carefully. Thank goodness, the walls and furniture stayed still. Now she had an urgent need to locate the bathroom, if she could just find her way to it...

That was easy enough. This was not a large flat, and everything was logically laid out. Kitchen over there, and that door led to John's bedroom, where presumably he was still indulging in the sleep of the just.

Splashing her face in cold water, Erinna became aware of a niggling irritation. Yes, he had been tactful in his delvings, and kind—almost tender—in his ministrations. But he was so—so wise, so *controlled*! When she allowed herself to remember it, she felt more resentment than gratitude. Layers of her, peeled away like that, with such low-key expertise, she had hardly noticed a thing.

She confronted her face in the mirror. What an appalling sight! Had she looked as bad as this last night? No man had ever seen her in such a state, let alone been permitted to share the causes of it. What an embarrassment! And why, breaking the habit of a lifetime, did she have to break it with the lofty Bryce, of all people?

She stared down at the enormous brown pullover. Then she lifted it up and studied the clinging scrap of silk beneath. In the harsh light of morning, it seemed faintly satirical—inadequate, saying nothing real about the woman inside, as if she wore it like a stage costume rather than a sign of her true personality. She shared a wry grin with her reflection. The combination of John's practical sweater and that glamorous dress struck her as comically ridiculous.

Her feet were bare, save for the sheer tights, now badly snagged. John must have removed her shoes when he'd tucked her up for the night; or, more likely, she'd removed them herself, earlier on. She recalled nothing about that, except this all-engulfing exhaustion. She should be glad, of course, that her shoes were *all* John had removed. After all, he'd had her at such a vulnerable disadvantage, he might have tried anything—achieved anything. But, even before that, he'd made no attempt to remove any garment. On the contrary, he'd quite deliberately wrapped her in acres of cosy brown wool. No, not the merest hint of a proposition, not the subtlest invasion of her feminine privacy... the perfect gentleman, from start to finish.

Yes, she should be glad, and naturally she was. So why was her relief tinged with this creeping regret, as if she had been betrayed, rather than respected? Was it simply a reaction to opening her innermost self to him, in that abnormal way? Wasn't there something more, an emptiness, a deprivation, in among its murky depths?

Erinna ran a basinful of warm water and began, very methodically, to soap her hands. Time enough for the rest of her when she got back to the house-block. She could have a shower, scour her body from head to toe, and perhaps her mind at the same time. Meanwhile, this would have to do.

She pulled out the plug and dried her hands on John's towel. Then she lifted the sweater again, and this time the dress as well, reaching to unhook the back fastening. She ran her own clean, smooth hands over her own soft, smooth skin, tracing the neat roundness of her waist, the full, firm curves of her breasts, the erect nipples. It was all her, the solid reality of her. No man had ever claimed or charted it. During her brief adulthood, she'd thought she had wanted them to, several of them. But none had ever got close enough, because—as John had so sagely pointed out last night—she'd never really invited them.

Her instincts were all mixed-up: natural sexuality with profound suspicion. Hardly surprising, when the roots of it were exposed, but deeply confusing all the same.

Now, this morning, here was the nicest irony yet! She'd actually spent a whole night alone with a man—or that was how the world would construe it, if the world ever got to hear of it. Come the dawn, and she was intact as ever—physically, at any rate—and confused as ever. More confused, because that man was John Bryce, not even on her male target list. Her feelings about him had been reliably cynical, but they must have undergone some strange shifts. Otherwise, how to explain this crazy twist? This crazy sense of loss, of insult, in the face of his admirable restraint?

'Casey,' she admonished herself, 'you're a case.'

Her hands moved on down, to the generous contours of her hips, the mound of her abdomen, the strong, white thighs, so sensual, so silken. Centres of pleasure in themselves, and leading the way to the secret centre of her, the core, where no alien trespasser had been, except in her more X-certificate dreams.

She was an enigma to herself. She had no idea what she wanted. She ought to be locked up! It was all impossibly bewildering. She should concentrate on work, the intellectual stuff she was really good at, and leave all this passion and drama to the experts.

Except the theatrical kind of drama—she wasn't giving that up, not for anyone. There might be problems ahead, adjusting to the new basis of her relationship with Anthony, the new honesty with John, but that just hardened her determination to make a success of Beatrice.

Padding past John's bedroom, she noticed his door was ajar. All these hours, they'd been in even closer proximity than she'd realised: a few yards apart, with only open doors between.

On impulse, she gave it a slight push. It swung in at once, leaving a gap easily wide enough for her to peep round. Exactly why, she never fully understood, but the next moment she found herself peeping.

The room was small, dominated by the single bed. John lay sprawled across the full length and width of it, his arms flung up and out, breathing peacefully, for all the world like an innocent infant at rest. Hair unkempt, features in repose; cheeks and chin roughly shadowed with the twenty-four-hour growth of beard.

Obviously he had felt hot in the night, because he had kicked his duvet into a crumpled heap round his feet. Like reluctant iron filings to a powerful magnet, Erinna's gaze travelled from his face to his chest—broad, darkened with hair—then down the rest of his body: slim torso, muscular legs . . .

Dr John Bryce lay before her, naked as the day he was born. And no less vulnerable, in his way, than she had been to him the evening before.

Erinna had younger brothers. Of course she knew how the male of the species was built; nevertheless, she might have expected to experience a certain impact at this sight, grabbing her attention without warning. But there was no way she was prepared for the total shock which seized her now.

His exposed masculinity was so different! So uncom-promising! Thrusting, threatening—yet wonderfully, paradoxically familiar, as if she'd been waiting to discover it. The missing piece in a puzzle, the positive to her negative...

Erinna allowed herself to stare freely at John Bryce, in all his unprotected prime and glory. Her whole being was concentrated into those ten seconds. Her mind, heart and body were equally, intimately involved in the sensations. She felt the changes, the movements, in all three, even as she gazed.

John grunted and sighed, as if he sensed the intensity of female eyes upon his bare flesh. Then he turned on his side, away from Erinna. The spell was cracked, the moment past. Erinna jerked her gaze from him, guilty as a child caught stealing apples. But her body was immobile, insisting on staying a minute longer. Now she glanced around the rest of the room, noting its sparse, almost spartan, order. One wall half covered with books—inevitable extensions of the man. Everything else kept to a simple minimum, except...

Except the one framed photograph which stood on the dresser. Erinna focused her eyes on its contents. A woman, yes, a smiling brunette, probably about thirty. Flanked by two beautiful, dark children. Erinna screwed her eyes up tighter. Surely it wasn't her imagination? Didn't they bear a more than passing resemblance to John? The nose on that older one—a girl, if she wasn't mistaken—and the way the hair grew on that little boy, and something in their expressions?

Erinna's emotions seethed, and twisted into a taut knot. Could this be his major commitment? The justifiable reason for his regular weekends away? Could that woman be the mother of his offspring; those the hands responsible for knitting him this cuddly creation Erinna was now wearing?

John Bryce, family man. Such a straightforward explanation for his ambivalent attitude to Erinna; why hadn't she thought of it before? The mature fluency with which he could take her in his arms, automatically comforting, accustomed to such warm contact—yet his ability to keep a strict distance, to withstand any sharper temptation when it arose. A vital ability, with that neat little unit at stake—its happiness, its cohesion, its future...

The digital alarm clock beside John's bed flashed seven-thirteen, catching Erinna's agitated eye. Early for a Sunday, especially after a late night. No one much would be around. She must slip away, now, right now, back to the ordinary seclusion of her own den, just a few hundred yards along the road. Right now, before John awoke, before anyone saw her, before this new surge of feeling had time to make too much sense of itself.

She pulled his door to, exactly as she had found it. She tiptoed to his living-room, folded his quilt and straightened his sofa. Then she retrieved her shoes and carried them to his front door, where she slipped them on and let herself quickly out into the fresh grey of a February morning.

At the tutorial on Monday, John sat deliberately out of Erinna's direct field of vision. It was painfully obvious, to Erinna at least, that he addressed her only when necessary, and kept the discussion running along studious, academic lines. It was the driest, edgiest hour she had ever spent, and she was heartily glad to escape at the end of it.

Thank God for her two companions, who diluted the atmosphere! If they noticed any new tension stretched between their tutor and their colleague, they never mentioned it. Both Erinna and John were so well able to master their behaviour, on the outside, it would have taken a very close acquaintance or a very perceptive observer to pick up that taut thread which linked them; tauter than ever, since yesterday.

Tuesday evening brought the next hurdle, in the shape of the next rehearsal. A double challenge for Erinna, with Anthony to confront as well as John. When it came to the point, she found the former much easier. After all, Anthony had never really suspected the extent of her private yearnings in his direction, and he surely would never guess her recent discovery about him. If she summoned up all her spirit, and her talent—self-discipline Bryce had called it—she shouldn't have too much trouble adding this extra level to her performance.

In the event, she excelled herself. Everyone was moved by Beatrice's developing awareness of her love for this long-standing antagonist, Benedick. At the end of the 'Kill Claudio' scene, she received a spontaneous ovation from the assembled cast, a hug from Anthony, and even an approving nod from the great director himself, with perhaps just a touch of deeper understanding—the barest twitch of a supportive smile?

Apart from that moment, John remained aloof, dealing with her only in a strictly practical vein, when the play's progress demanded. In his approach to the rest of the company he was relaxing further each week— but tonight, with Erinna, he reverted to his old brusque self. This time, the others *did* notice, and sent glances and nudges towards her; but Erinna held on to her dignity, acting for all she was worth—for her own benefit, and Anthony's, and John Bryce's. Really, when it came down to it, Shakespeare hardly had a look-in this evening!

John was evidently regretting Saturday night's escapade as much as she was. More, to judge by his demeanour. Erinna was sorry about that, but there was nothing she could do. She wouldn't mind rolling back the film herself, but the thing had happened, and that was that.

Surely John wasn't concerned that she planned to make something of it, hold it against him, that lapse into humanity? Use it, somehow, to undermine his professional or personal status? Remind him of it at uncomfortable moments?

If so, he was not the intuitive man she had thought he was. Erinna had had this feeling he knew her, through and through, by some unfathomable instinct; now it seemed he hardly knew her at all, and didn't particularly want to, either.

At long last the session was over, and for once Erinna was first to grab her coat and head for the exit.

'Hey, Erinna!'

Anthony caught her arm. She smiled round at him as serenely as she could. 'Oh, goodnight, Anthony!'

'Not coming to the Union? It isn't very late.' He seemed a bit surprised, perhaps even piqued by her uncharacteristic coolness.

'I'm bushed. I think I'll give it a miss tonight.'

'Not surprising you're tired. You were brilliant, Erinna. I mean, you're always great, but—well, I won't even ask what's got into you tonight!' He hesitated, and when she could only manage a strained smile, he continued, 'As for John, he's a magician! You never did a better day's work than when you charmed him into taking us on. The whole of Dramsoc is in your debt, love.'

What a time to choose to make his first real acknowledgement of her effort in securing John's services! And no doubt he was only doing it now because he felt uneasy at her new objectivity.

Erinna hoped her smile was natural enough to re-assure him. 'It was nothing,' she lied. 'But now you must excuse me, Anthony...'

'Great dance we had,' he interrupted. He really was insecure, she realised—eager to restore the two of them to their former footing. 'I looked out for you later, for another one, but you'd vanished. Fairy coach whisk you away, did it, on the chime of midnight?'

'I left quite soon after our dance, actually. I had a headache.' Once you started glibly lying, it became simpler to carry on. 'I'm never much good at that loud disco stuff, and the smoke, and those lights seem to...'

'Pity, though. We must catch up with our encore another time. See you, then, Erinna. Get a good kip, you look a bit pale.'

'See you, Anthony!'

'We can't risk losing our perfect Beatrice!' he called, as she reached the door.

She waved vaguely over her shoulder and fled out into the night. Safely there, she sucked in draughts of cold air. None of this was going to be simple. Nothing was ever simple. At least she was learning to recognise and accept that much reality.

She set off for her Hall at a brisk walk. Half a minute later, she knew there were faster footsteps behind her. Even as she braced herself to hear it, John's voice joined them.

'Erinna, stop! Wait!'

She neither stopped nor waited. She walked on at exactly the same pace.

'Erinna!' Catching up effortlessly, he fell into step beside her.

'I want to get back to my room,' she informed him, staring ahead.

'And so you shall.'

'Thank you, kind sir.' She sank into sarcasm. All right for him to be so cheery, now no one else was here to listen and watch! So, he was just guarding his reputation—it was everyone *else's* opinion that mattered, was it? How pathetic! A man like him should surely have the courage and integrity to...

'I won't detain you from your beauty sleep more than a minute. I've got something important to say, but it won't take long.'

Erinna halted abruptly, wheeling to face him. As if he had expected it, John stopped to confront her at precisely the same moment.

'I suppose I ought to thank you for your hospitality on Saturday night,' she managed to croak. 'Your help and—and the loan of your sofa.' It was less than she should be saying, but absolutely the most she could bring herself to utter.

His smile was a gleam of teeth in the darkness. 'There's no need to thank me.' The smile evaporated. 'No need to feel embarrassed, either, Erinna. Or regretful, or whatever it is you're feeling. You've got nothing to regret. Your secrets are safe with me. I respect your privacy.'

His tone had dropped to that low sensitivity she hadn't heard since three nights ago; the one which had touched layers of her emotional self, never uncovered before. 'I'm not regretting it, John.' This was scarcely true, so she looked him in the eye all the more defiantly. 'I get the impression *you* are, though?'

'Me?' He ran a hand through his hair. He was certainly weary—perhaps stressed—but if he could keep up this jocular style, so could she. 'No, I'm not regretting it, not exactly... Look, I don't want to talk about it now, any more than you do. This isn't the time or place. But there's this one thing I must ask you before...'

'Your sweater!'

'I beg your pardon?'

'You'll be wanting your sweater back, of course! And your hanky!' How stupid of her, not to remember, when she had them neatly washed and folded, waiting for a suitably discreet opportunity to be returned to their rightful owner. So far, such an opportunity had eluded her, and she'd forgotten all about them.

He was chuckling. 'Oh! No, not those. To tell you the truth, they'd slipped my mind.'

'Oh.' So it wasn't those. What could it be, then?

'When I surfaced on Sunday morning, to find my house guest had sneaked away like a thief in the night, I was more concerned about her than any of my possessions she might have adopted. Inadvertently or otherwise.' He grew serious. 'It's OK, Erinna, you can return them any time.'

'They're all ready. Shall I bring them to the seminar on Thursday? Anonymously disguised in a carrier bag, of course.'

'Never mind what you wrap them in, it's not likely to fool anyone into believing it's your essay on Elizabeth Barrett Browning,' he observed. 'You might as well hand them over and be damned. Yes, Thursday will be fine.'

'Right. And thanks again for the loan. You probably saved me from a severe attack of chilblains, at the very least.'

It all sounded so superficial, so flip! So far removed from the true total of his effect on her that night!

'I've told you, you were welcome.' John seemed to be studying her closely now, as if to fathom her real responses rather than these self-consciously wooden ones.

The harder he stared, the more she resolved not to display them. He'd pierced quite far enough into her already. 'What was this question, then? Because I really do want to get back to my room.'

'Ah, yes.' He shook himself, visibly, back to action. 'What are your plans for this coming weekend?'

'You *what*?'

It was an ungainly reply, lamentably low on poise, but she couldn't help that. Whatever possibilities she might have predicted, this was not among them. From his manner she had expected something quite prosaic—about work, or the play—but this?

'Next weekend,' he repeated laboriously, as if for an idiot's benefit. 'They often begin on a Friday evening. In three days' time.' He held three fingers in front of her nose. 'Are you busy, Erinna? Booked?'

'Well, not really, but...'

'Then could you spare me a day of your life?'

'A day?' She knew she was being gormless, but this was all so unlikely, she couldn't get to grips with it.

'In the twenty-four-hour sense of the word. Let's say, Friday afternoon to Saturday evening?'

Now Erinna actually stepped back, gaping like a fish. 'You mean, go *away*? With *you*?'

'This is not so much a proposition,' he assured her, 'as an invitation.'

'To do what?'

'It's not so much a matter of *doing*, as *going*. You won't be called upon to *do* anything—unless you choose to, of course.' It was too dark to see the teasing glint in his eye, but she heard it in his voice.

It was a struggle to keep the agitated squeak out of her own voice. 'Well then, where would I be called upon to *go*? And why?'

'I'm sorry, I can't tell you that. Look upon it as a mystery tour.' Sensing her expression of pure paranoia, John reached over to lay a light hand on her shoulder. 'Listen, Erinna, it would ruin the point if I spell it out for you beforehand. But I'll tell you this much, if it helps you to make up your mind. It would involve a motorway drive, late Friday afternoon. Then a simple meal in a bistro I know. Then the main event, which I can't divulge, for reasons which will become clear in the fullness of time.'

'And then?' Erinna was strung out with curiosity, but she was too cautious to let that win the day, yet.

'How do you mean—and then?'

'Where do we spend the night, if we're not coming back here after this main event?'

'Ah, the night!' He regarded her gravely. 'We spend it somewhere quietly comfortable, at no risk to either of our virtues.'

'I didn't mean that,' she snapped, unconvincingly.

'There would be separate accommodation, and assorted chaperons in attendance,' he told her, with mock pomposity.

She stared at him, nonplussed. Quiet and comfortable? Assorted chaperons? Surely he must mean his own domestic arrangements? The wife, or whoever she was, and kids, in that stylishly framed photograph. Was this a complicated, tactful—and particularly nerve-racking—way of telling her the truth about his personal life? How should she react?

'So, are we on?' He was being remarkably patient, really, but it was growing steadily colder, and so was Erinna, and standing about in the icy dark just wasn't enhancing her decision-making faculty.

'I'm sorry, John, I'm seizing up. I really must keep moving.'

She marched on again, and he strode beside her. Suddenly, she demanded, 'Is it the same place you usually go to at weekends?'

He was apparently primed for this one. 'Could be.'

She must not become exasperated! He was doing it on purpose!

'This main event—is it a show of some kind, or what?'

He considered. 'Of some kind,' he conceded, generously.

She glanced round at him, but she continued walking. 'You've got no intention of letting on any more than you have, have you, John?'

'That's right, Erinna.'

'If I come, I'll find out the rest for myself? And if...'

'If you don't, you probably never will,' he agreed calmly.

They walked on in silence. Erinna's block loomed only yards away. She fought a spasm of sick panic. 'Do I have to decide now?'

It was John's turn to halt and swing round, right in her path. 'If you need time to think, maybe that should be your answer. Maybe I only want your company if you know you really want to come.'

It was a new challenge, delivered on a new, harsher note. And he just might be right, at that. Erinna had never been one to dither, so why do it now? If she went, God knew what she might be letting herself in for, but at least she'd find out, eventually. If she refused, John might never repeat the offer, whatever it was.

'Fair enough,' she said. 'I can take a risk as well as anyone.' Unconsciously, she drew herself up, meeting his eyes and his terms on equal grounds. 'Thank you for your invitation, John. I accept.'

Now he softened. His whole attitude melted: tone, expression, even the way he was standing. One arm reached to her again, the hand brushing a soft tendril from her brow, then tracing the curve of her cheek, fore-finger lingering down her nose, mouth and chin—almost absent-mindedly, as if following its own instinct rather than any dictate from his head.

Then he dropped his hand to his side, as if recalling himself.

'I'm glad. I'm very glad, Erinna. And I do realise you see it as a big risk. You're right, it *is* a risk. I hope you won't live to regret taking it.' They shared a brief silence, before he added, 'You might be in for one or two surprises, but I hope they won't be entirely unpleasant.'

'So do I.'

'Hmmm.' He was cagey again. 'I have a feeling you'll cope.'

'Cope?' This sounded ominous.

'Some people find *all* surprises difficult,' he explained.

'Hmmm,' Erinna echoed, wishing she wasn't one of them. Then she grew businesslike. 'My last lecture on Friday's over by four. I could be ready to leave at half-past.'

'That sounds ideal. We'll finalise it on Thursday, shall we? After the seminar? Now, hadn't you better get in there before we both solidify, or catch our death? Or is this a subtle tactic to ensure we have to call the trip off anyway?'

He swivelled her round and gave her a gentle shove towards the building. Erinna turned to stare at him, fighting a twinge of resentment, then she smiled and nodded.

'OK then, John.'

'Sleep tight!' he called, as she left him.

And you! But her reply was silent, drowned in the flood of this powerful image his words conjured up. A stark, almost tangible, vision of a naked man, abandoned in satisfying sleep.

CHAPTER EIGHT

JOHN BRYCE and his car enjoyed an excellent relationship. They covered hundreds of miles together most weekends, so it was important for both of them to be dependable, comfortable and efficient.

Erinna watched John covertly now from the passenger seat. Behind the wheel, as everywhere else, he was fully in charge. Competent, with a natural authority offset by that rebellious streak. They were fifteen minutes down the motorway, and he kept in the fast lane, just above the legal speed limit. His driving made her feel secure, yet exhilarated. He never took chances, but he always took opportunities. *Down* the motorway—yes, they were travelling south, that much she had gleaned. Probably bound for London—that would fit in—nearly two hundred miles in this direction, and the most likely home of culture or entertainment, or whatever this main event turned out to be...

Erinna stifled another surge of nervous impatience, staring out of her window at a landscape of drab greens and browns, not long before a wintry dusk. John was not the man to make polite conversation for its own sake anywhere, least of all when controlling a powerful car. He had greeted her, briskly amiable, checked that she was ready and happy to be off, and that was that. Now he seemed preoccupied—with more than the demands of fast driving, surely? In this mood he was unapproachable and, anyway, Erinna had preoccupations of her own.

She glanced at his profile: eyes steady on the road, just as his hands were steady on gearstick and wheel. His long mouth was set firm, chin jutting in concentration, dark hair falling over high, wide brow. To Erinna, it was all warmly familiar, even as it was still alien.

Why did everything about John produce this instant conflict in her? He was so reinforcing and right, slotting into her life—so frightening and fierce, disrupting it. Her own feelings for him, unchained without warning, were fierce and frightening enough. These last few days, it was as if a screen had been torn down, revealing her real self to that other self—that struggling Erinna, searching vainly for some impossible combination of passion with safety.

John Bryce had become, mysteriously, necessary; a prerequisite to existence. It was no good lecturing herself not to be obsessive, extravagant, over the top. In her heart, she knew it to be true. She had to rely on instinct rather than experience in these matters, but she trusted instinct not to mislead her.

Now she stretched, settling herself lower in the upholstered seat. Shared car journeys were such strange contradictions. You were intimately trapped together in this little metal container, yet stuck out in the big world, far from anywhere or anyone you recognised, mutually braving the dangers of the open road. Close, safe, yet always threatened—which, in a way, summed up how she felt about John.

She sighed. Why beat about the bush? She was falling in love with this man. Not those ethereal yearnings she'd wallowed in before, but a deep, dark joy, twisted up with a physical, emotional pain. And wasn't that inevitable, her mind nagged, from the moment she'd understood how unattainable he was? A hint of those personal com-

mitments—a glimpse into that tender sensitivity underlying his nature—and wham! She was hooked! Same old
story, same old contrary...

'All right, Erinna?'

She started out of her private reverie. Fortunately, he
was too busy surveying the road to catch her blush. 'Yes,
thanks—why?'

'That was a heartfelt sigh. Need to stop for air, or
anything?'

'No, really, I'm fine.'

Now he did glance round at her, with a quick grin.
'Fine, but in an agony of tenterhooks, eh?'

'Just pleasant anticipation,' she retorted, assuming a
nonchalance which fooled neither of them.

'I admire you, you know,' he said abruptly.

'Admire?' She looked sharply at him, then in the opposite direction.

'Admire, yes, and respect. Not everyone would take
on a challenge like this.'

Her blush deepened. Curses on her red hair and delicate skin! Curses on him, for touching all her most re-
sponsive nerves!

'Not everyone would invite them to,' she replied, rather
primly.

'That's true enough.' He frowned into his driving
mirror before pulling out to overtake a convoy of three
cumbersome lorries. Into the outside lane, past the ob-
stacles, back in the fast centre lane, using the motorway
as it was designed to be used. Calmly doing it right,
getting the best out of the situation, expending as much
energy as required, no more and no less. The man in a
nutshell.

'Not everyone pushes people as hard as I do,' he was
saying. 'I expect you resent me bitterly, Erinna? I expect
you think I'm a ruthless, arrogant bastard?'

'I...' I did once, but now... 'I think that's one of your images,' she said, after careful thought.

'Images?'

'Masks,' she declared without hesitation.

His eyebrows arched. 'You see it as a mask?'

It was an echo, a reflection rather than a question, but Erinna answered it anyway. 'I do—now.'

Disconcertingly, perhaps ruefully, he chuckled. 'There was I, probing your soft inner recesses, while kidding myself I was maintaining my own mystique—and there were you, effortlessly penetrating it.'

Erinna wished he would refrain from using these double-edged expressions. His closeness, its effect on her senses, was overwhelming enough without these verbal embellishments.

'I don't know about effortlessly,' she remarked.

After a short silence, John changed tack. 'You know, I've never asked where you live? Your family, I mean.'

'In the Wirral, not far from Liverpool. My mother wanted to stay within easy reach of Ireland, even though she didn't want to live there any more. Also, she had an aunt and uncle who lived in Cheshire at the time, but they moved away soon after that.'

John nodded. 'Not too far for you to go home, then, from college?'

'That's right. That was partly why I applied to Mid-Anglia.' She paused. 'Actually, I don't go back very often. Sometimes I don't even go in the vacations. Some of my friends have a house, off campus, so I stay there and find work locally. The grant never goes far enough, and there's none to spare at home, and anyway it's getting to be such a squash. It's only a small house, and all the kids are growing up...I have to share a bedroom with two sisters, and...'

'And you've got used to your privacy and peace?'

'I love them all dearly, of course, but yes—I do find it a bit stifling. I don't think I add much to their life any more. Mum likes to know I'm alive and well, and reasonably happy in what I'm doing, but she doesn't need to see me more than once in a while.'

John was sympathetic. 'It's only normal, reaching a stage when you want to flee the nest, however comfortable the nest. My personal observations of parenthood are limited to a younger generation, but I can imagine both sides must be heartily glad to snatch a bit of space, once the offspring achieves independence.'

This reference to parenthood was cryptic, but it was the closest he had yet come to a piece of direct information. Erinna swallowed hard to clear a tightness in her throat, then shifted the subject sideways, to less of a potential minefield.

'Do you come from a large family, John?'

'Not particularly. I'm the middle one of three. Older brother, emigrated to New Zealand years ago, doing well in business, I hear. Younger sister, also an academic— in fact, a rising star, lecturing in law—very much the modern career woman. Yeats wouldn't approve.'

'Oh, yes?' If he was fishing for a stock feminist reaction, he was out of luck. Erinna didn't feel like giving him the satisfaction; in any case, she was interested to find out more about him. 'And your parents? Are they still alive?'

'Very much so—alive and kicking.'

'Where?'

He hesitated before replying, and when he did, it was with a slight smile. 'Across the water.'

'You mean, in America?'

'No.' The smile was distinctly ironic.

'Canada?'

'Those are across the *pond*, not the water,' John pointed out, emphasising a transatlantic drawl.

Light was beginning to dawn. Erinna's gaze was wide on his face. 'You mean, in *Ireland*?'

'I do. Eire, as ever was. Cork, to be precise.'

'But why didn't you *say*? Have they always lived there? Does that make you Irish?'

John changed gear in order to overtake again, and she was forced to wait a full minute for his answer. When it came, it was solemn and straightforward. 'I didn't tell you, Erinna, because I don't like anyone knowing too much about me. Call it part of my mask, if you like. Yes, they have always lived there. And yes, that does make me Irish. Years of globe-trotting, especially in the States, have blunted my accent and broadened my horizons, but on my passport, and in my soul, I'm a pure-blooded Celt, as much as you.'

'Probably more than me.' Erinna was digesting this revelation. It explained a lot; that empathy, which had always flowed between them, even through the antagonism, was traceable now, quite simply, to shared roots. 'I haven't lived there since I was ten, don't forget. Thirteen years, more than half my life. I'm sure you stayed much longer than that?'

'I went to university there,' he agreed, 'before moving on to Cambridge, then Yale, for my higher qualifications. But I've got a few years on you,' he reminded her. 'If I left when I was twenty-one, I reckon we both deserted the old country about the same time.'

Erinna considered this, appreciating the symmetry of it. Strange, too, to think of him as a young adult when she was just a little girl, not even adolescent. The difference a decade could make, and yet now...

'Do you go back much to see them?' she wondered.

'Whenever I can, yes. I go back quite a lot. I still identify with the place. Wherever I go, whatever I do, I still *feel* Irish.'

'I know exactly what you mean—a kind of folk memory.' Erinna's own memory was throwing out some action replays. 'No wonder you had so much to say about Yeats! You really should have told me, John!'

'I'm glad you can laugh.' John was wry. 'You weren't deeply amused at the time.'

Erinna felt peculiarly liberated. Some people find all surprises unpleasant, he had said. If all this weekend's surprises were as positive as this one, she was sure she could cope.

'But that seems ages ago. I feel as if I've gone through months, even years, since then—not just a few weeks.'

'Learning's never a constant flow,' John observed. 'It comes in fits and starts.'

Today's Erinna was content to accept his words of wisdom without protest. She knew they were true, and she sensed he was applying them to himself, as much as to her.

They were now north of Birmingham, where two motorways diverged. Erinna confidently expected them to head east, crossing to the M1 and London, but she was wrong. John was in lane for the M5, signed south-west.

'We're not going to Wales, are we? Cardiff, or...?'

'Could be.'

'Bristol? Bath?'

'Why not?' He smiled wickedly at her.

'You'd make a great resistance fighter,' she grumbled. 'Never crack under pressure.'

'You call this pressure? Believe me, Erinna, I'd be as feeble as the next man, in the face of torture.'

Somehow, Erinna doubted that, but she kept her opinion to herself.

Just after seven o'clock they were pulling into the centre of Bristol.

'I knew it!' Erinna crowed.

'Your deductive powers are remarkable, Miss Casey. Small wonder you propound such excellent literary arguments.'

'I hardly know Bristol at all. I did come here once, to visit a friend, but I didn't see much of it really.' She was gazing out at the neon-lit streets, a lively urban evening scene like any other.

'It's a fine city, but you're not likely to see much more of it on this visit, because we're heading for the suburbs later.'

The suburbs. Where people lived, and had homes and families. 'And first?'

'First, we're going to Clifton.'

'Clifton? I'm sure I remember that. Where the Downs are, and the fantastic suspension bridge? Yes, I went there.'

'Right—and the University, and the Zoo, and a good few stately Victorian residences, with trendy un-Victorian residents . . . and fancy shops, and restaurants, and . . . by the way, are you hungry?'

'Starving,' she admitted.

'I promised you a bistro supper, and . . .' he swung the car off the main road, along a side street, then into another small turning ' . . . we're almost there.'

The place was friendly and unassuming, belying high standards of food and service. Tucking into *paté maison*, followed by vegetarian stuffed aubergine, Erinna tried to feel philosophical about the way the *patron* greeted John like an old friend, while casting inquisitive glances at Erinna. It all fitted, only too well. Here was this established, respected customer, known locally as a family man, accompanied by an unidentified young woman. No more than a few miles from his own doorstep, if Erinna's hunches were right. She couldn't really blame the *patron* if he eyed her suspiciously.

She was on the point of broaching the topic at last, despite all her firm intentions to stay cool—to show John she could bide her time as long as he liked. But he had loosened up himself now; chatting to her amicably over his steak *au poivre* as he replenished their glasses with a rich *vin rouge*. She had to admire the poise, the sheer gall of the man. Away from the University and its restrictions, he was relaxed and expansive. Yes, almost charming. This suggestion of a suave sophistication unnerved Erinna more than anything else had yet.

If only it wasn't for this uncertainty about the rest of the evening, not to mention the night...

'There's time for a dessert, if you like. We don't have to be anywhere till about nine.' He waved a hand at the well-stocked trolley. 'Or I saw a perfect piece of Camembert on the cheeseboard, if you...'

'No, thanks, John. But it was delicious. This is just my sort of place.'

'I thought it might be.' John leaned back, smiling across at her.

'Have you—have you known it long?' The simplest questions were the most significant, the trickiest to ask.

'Oh, years, on and off. Since André and Jack started up—let me see—must have been in the mid-seventies. I often come when I'm in the area.'

'Are you in the area most weekends?'

It was a brave venture, but it backfired. 'That would be telling.'

She tried again. 'Where we're going next, is it far?'

'Not at all. A quarter of a mile, or less—easy walking distance. That's why,' he confided, draining his glass, 'I'm indulging in more than half of this carafe of house red. I haven't got to drive anywhere for a few hours. In fact...' he turned to signal to André '...I think I'll have a cognac. Would you join me?'

'No, really. A cup of coffee would be lovely, but that's all.'

Stepping out, away from the secure glow of candle-light and company, Erinna wound her scarf snugly round her neck. This was a damp, chill air; you could feel and smell the sea in it.

All at once she felt cold and alone, in this unknown city, with this unknown quantity, embarking on an unknown experience. She shivered, and shoved her hands in her pockets. John had told her not to dress up, and he was certainly informal himself in his usual lean jeans, thick shirt and jacket. She had opted for plaid trousers and a green cableknit sweater, but she had decided to wear her best coat rather than the old padded anorak, and she was sure there was a pair of woollen gloves here in the pockets...

Her shiver had not escaped John. His arm came round her now to draw her close, transmitting warmth and support as he walked beside her. It was the first time he had touched her today, and Erinna had to summon every ounce of will-power simply to keep on the move.

She had imagined their destination must be a theatre of some kind, but again she was wrong. It was a pub. Just an ordinary pub, on a corner between two streets in an ordinary residential area, among shops and houses. Quite a large pub, full of ordinary locals, socialising on a Friday night.

Or was it so ordinary? Erinna gazed around, slightly bemused, as she followed John through the lobby. One side of the entrance, her eye lit on a poster, fixed to the wall.

'Poetry reading upstairs tonight,' announced a bold sticker plastered across the top of it. Underneath, in smaller print, Erinna got as far as, 'Our regular poetry recital will take place on the third Friday of the month, as usual. February's contributors will include...'

'John! Wait!' She grabbed at his arm, as he strode purposefully into the lounge bar.

'What?' He turned. 'Come on, we'll be late!'

Now they'd arrived, he had become unaccountably tense. But Erinna refused to be dragged past this vital clue. 'Just let me see this, John, please! Is it what we've come for...let me *see*!'

He stood by with an air of resignation, watching as she read on, her mutterings punctuated with a crescendo of squeaks.

'It *is*! It's tonight! This is what you've brought me here for, isn't it? But why—who's on? Hmmm, I don't know much about her, I think she's American... Oh yes, *he's* that Nigerian who won a prize, I remember reading some of his... Hey, look! *Look!*' She confronted John. Her expression, her whole being, were alight.

'I'm looking,' John assured her.

'Guest of honour, Devin O'Connor!'

She could only just squeeze the words out, she was so excited.

'You don't say!' But her enthusiasm had infected John's smile.

'It says here, "Guest of honour, Devin O'Connor"!'

He peered over her shoulder. 'It certainly does,' he agreed.

'John, I never expected—I mean, I just couldn't guess where we were going, but I'd never have worked this out in a million years!'

'I don't suppose you would.' He was enjoying this, now the cat was out of the bag.

'It was a brilliant idea, absolutely brilliant! How did you know he was on here tonight? Do you often come to these?'

He shrugged. 'Now and again. It came to my attention, and of course I immediately thought of you.'

'But why couldn't you *tell* me? Why all the cloak and dagger bit?'

'I had my reasons. Anyway, you loved it really. Go on, Erinna, admit you did—admit the mystery was more than half the anticipation.'

'Well, I don't know. I might have refused to come, and then I'd have missed it and never have known...' Her heart sank, even to think of such a possibility. 'But I accepted! Thank you, John!'

'I wasn't pulling the strings,' John pointed out. 'It *was* you who accepted, on your own account. And anyway,' he added drily, 'you haven't actually heard anything yet.'

'But I'm going to!' Devin O'Connor, in person! What would he be like? 'He's last on the programme, but we mustn't miss any... Hey, look, it started at eight-thirty, not nine! Come on, we'd better get in there!'

Now it was her turn to march ahead, leading John through the lounge and out the other side as she followed a series of signs and arrows. He followed meekly, across a hall, up some shabbily carpeted stairs, across another hall... yes, here it was! Quite a big room, surprisingly packed with culture-seekers; its atmosphere dense with the blend of intellect and emotion that constitutes poetry.

They slipped in at the back and stood leaning against the wall. There was hardly a free chair to be had, and even then not without pushing along rows and disturbing intent listeners. Erinna might have tried, but John seemed loath to attract attention. There might be people in here who knew him, and Erinna's presence might spark off undesirable gossip.

But she soon banished such speculation to the back of her mind, giving herself up to the sheer pleasure of words, and the ideas, the sensations they could weave. The American woman was well under way, up at the front, and Erinna liked what she was hearing. It was accessible, without being trite. Some of the themes rang sympathetic bells in Erinna's female heart and head.

She almost forgot John until the selection was over and the poetess sat down to warm applause. Then, amid a general bustle, Erinna realised that several spectators were turning in their seats, looking about, spotting John and waving. He smiled back, but made no effort to communicate further; in fact, it seemed to Erinna, he exuded an air of 'leave me alone' which would be hard to ignore. Certainly, no one approached him.

It was becoming clearer all the time that he was no stranger here, however much he tried to keep his profile low. But somehow, after this wonderful gesture, Erinna felt more ready to forgive him anything else.

The Nigerian read next, and again Erinna became absorbed in the mood spun by the words. A very different mood, very different words, but still with an appeal that was universal as well as specific—one of the arts of true poetry.

It was a short set, perhaps half an hour. Then there was another gap while people jostled, chatted, compared reactions, and went off to recharge their glasses.

Would the guest of honour be next? Erinna stared about the room, wondering if she could see him now, trying to envisage the flesh and blood man from the lines she knew so well on the flat page.

'Want a drink?' John whispered in her ear, as the compère—president of a regional Poetry Society, and *not* one of the world's natural public speakers—stood up to introduce the next artist.

'What? Oh, no, thanks!' At such a moment, he could think about such trivia as having a drink?

'And now,' the compère was saying diffidently, 'it gives me very great pleasure indeed to welcome back one of the top English language poets of our generation. I say English language because, of course, to describe him as English, or even British, would be no more accurate than it would have been for either of our last guests—which is why we invited them together, this evening. This one is Irish, through and through, and it's got to be our gain that he decides, for whatever reason, to write in our language. Ladies and gentlemen, I'm proud to present Devin O'Connor!'

Joining the burst of clapping, Erinna glanced round to make sure John was appreciating this historic occasion. Then she glanced again. He wasn't there!

He was slipping away from her, along the back wall. Erinna was aghast. Surely this need for a drink, or a call of nature, couldn't be more pressing than the event they were about to witness? She could not believe it—she absolutely couldn't!

'John!' she called softly.

He took no notice, but went on walking towards the door.

'John, you *can't* go now!' she implored.

Still he ignored her, and by this time the applause was dying down, and he would be out of earshot unless she raised her voice into the silence. She wasn't going to do that, so she shrugged and left him to his diversion, untimely as it was. She would never understand men. Coming all this way specially, then disappearing just before the climax of the evening!

She turned back to the low platform, where there was a chair as well as a lectern, so that the reader could choose whether to sit or stand. Had he arrived? No, not yet. The audience was quiet now, sharing a collective expectancy. Erinna felt breathless, like someone on the verge of meeting a fantasy lover, face to face, for the first time. Of course it was foolish, but perhaps she could allow her romantic urges one final fling before settling to serene maturity?

Out of a reluctant corner of her eye, she registered that John had not walked out of the door, but past it. Then on towards the front of the room. Then he was stepping up to the platform. As he entered the spotlight, he was taking a slim paperback volume from the inside pocket of his jacket. Erinna recognised it at once.

The applause began again, spontaneously, then died down into a hushed stillness. In that split second, Erinna's brain whirled like a roulette wheel, and came to rest in a new place—facing a new, incredible truth.

It had been like climbing a steep ladder. The evening's first surprise was that John Bryce was her compatriot. The evening's second surprise was that he had brought her here to watch and listen to her literary idol, Devin O'Connor.

The evening's third surprise was that John Bryce *was* Devin O'Connor.

The shock was so total, it was impossible to separate rapture from horror. A jumble of phrases—sentences—conversations flew back to Erinna's memory, pieces of puzzle darting about and settling into whole new shapes.

John Bryce was Devin O'Connor!

The full implications failed to reach Erinna's comprehension. It was too much to take in. The reality of it eluded her. She simply couldn't grasp it; all she could do was stand there, propped up by the back wall of that unfamiliar room, over an unfamiliar pub in the middle of Bristol, and do exactly what John Bryce had driven her all this way to do—hear the poet, Devin O'Connor, reading from his own work.

Erinna knew most of the poems as well as he did, maybe even better than he did, as if she'd written them herself. But now she drank in every syllable, every nuance, relating to it all over again on a new level. If it had made profound sense to her before, it was painfully, personally true now, delivered from the mouth of its creator. John Bryce, alias Devin O'Connor.

Understated as ever, he had chosen to sit. His voice carried clearly to the back of the room, without benefit of a microphone, yet he barely seemed to raise it above its normal low pitch. As he spoke, Erinna picked out the Irish lilt at the base of his accent, distinguishing it now from added layers of North American. It wasn't very strong, but it was undeniably there—just as hers was there. Two exiles from the same native land.

That same voice was wafted back to her mind's ear, from other times and places... 'Presumably O'Connor intends his stuff to be delivered in Irish cadences.' 'Never mistake illusion for the thing itself.' 'People are real, feelings are real, relationships are real, not just notions in your head—or mine—or Devin O'Connor's.'

Tonight he read 'Emerald I'll' and others in that group, rich in traditional Celtic lore, yet tight with vitriolic social and political comment. Then he read a series of lyrical love verses, which had always been Erinna's favourite. Now they were charged with such a depth and wealth of meaning, it was all she could do to choke back the tears; in fact, quite a few escaped, and she hoped no one noticed. Not tears of sweet, sentimental longing, but sharp pangs, a torment of real desire—a writhing of conflict.

Who were they addressed to, these beautiful messages she had so often recited to herself, knowing nothing of their originator or his private life? Now she did know him—be honest, now she loved him—how could she bear it, understanding they were for some other woman... always had been... worse, far worse, always would be?

Devin O'Connor had known loss, and passionate love, that much had been obvious to Erinna for years, ever since she'd discovered his work. It had never mattered, except that any poet's job was to involve his reader in the truth of his emotions and visions. If they failed to ring true, he had failed to do the job. O'Connor had, indisputably, done the job.

But now, here, there was more than the poet and his words in a book. There was the man. As Erinna watched and listened, it made perfect sense. The shock was wearing off, and suddenly it seemed logical, as if she had always known. Of *course* John Bryce was Devin O'Connor! How could it be any other way?

She cringed, remembering some of her own attacks on the unbending Dr Bryce. 'I don't know how you have the *nerve* to teach poetry at all!' she had ranted. 'You obviously wouldn't recognise real feeling if it rose up and hit you in the face!' she had taunted. 'People like you should be banned from having any connection with poetry!' she had carped. 'As if a man like you could *really* understand what poets are trying to say!' Oh, the irony, the supreme satire of all that!

Recalling it now was just too humiliating. Not that Erinna could have been expected to guess the truth. A rising resentment leavened her remorse. No doubt he had good reason for keeping his two identities so strictly apart, but was it quite fair that Erinna should be left feeling stunned and foolish as a result?

His set was coming to an end. The audience was rapt, but it had been an hour, and he was tired. Even from here, Erinna could clearly sense that weariness, like a tangible experience of her own. Underneath it, she also sensed his elation. He might be controlled, on the surface; he was not the man to wear his heart on his sleeve. But it was all there, in the poems, for those who cared to find it. Now he was happy to have shared them with a roomful of receptive fellow human beings. Erinna knew she had participated in a rare communal event.

Their response was exuberant. After repeated cries of 'Encore!', John gave them one more short piece—a touching ballad on the birth of a child. Erinna's feelings on hearing this one were so mixed, she thought she would explode. To discover so much about a man, to accept the rightness of his place in her heart, only to be told, simultaneously, that he belonged somewhere else! That his life consisted of a whole scenario of facts and loyalties which could never include her! It was cruel.

John had talked about learning. If learning had to consist of such agonising lessons, she could only hope she'd be spared much more of it.

This time his audience allowed him to sign off, and he sat quietly on his chair while the compère gave brief thanks to all the readers. Then, as everyone began to disperse, John stood and made his way, equally quietly, to where Erinna waited at the back of the room.

Suddenly she realised she was exhausted, and slumped on the nearest seat, vacated by a spectator making for the bar before closing time. John walked towards her, stopping now and then to exchange a quick word with an admirer, or perhaps an acquaintance—friendly and polite, but encouraging no one to chat. Then he was standing over her, the book of his poems still clutched in one hand, the other in his pocket.

There, among the crowd, they stared at one another. He was solemn, only his eyes revealing that inner elation. When he finally spoke, his voice was as low and as firm as ever.

'Well, Miss Casey?'

'Well, Mr O'Connor?'

He sat down on the next chair. Reaching over, he took her hand. He still did not smile, but there was a gentle humour in his expression.

'So, my chief scourge and self-appointed critic? Give it to me straight. Tell me just what you think of me. I can take it.'

Her hand was inert, paralysed within his. His thumb rubbed her palm, automatically it seemed, as he went on studying her face. Erinna wanted desperately to enfold him, to give herself up to him. To tell him how she gloried in his attainment, and her small reflected role in it. Instead, she looked down at their linked hands, then up into his shining eyes, searching for words to express even a fraction of her feelings.

'What do I think of you?' She blushed, then she smiled. 'You're a—a swarthy poet. That's what I think.'

CHAPTER NINE

THEY drove south, out of the city, through drizzle and solid darkness. John needed all his concentration to negotiate the fast road with its bends and hills.

To their right, that famous suspension bridge, vividly illuminated, spanned the dramatic Avon Gorge. Erinna twisted in her seat for a better view as they left it behind.

'Stunning sight, isn't it?'

John's eyes might be fixed ahead, but he knew what she was staring at. The sound of his words startled her. It was the first time either of them had spoken since leaving the pub, and now, suddenly, that voice—close, steady, personal, yet exactly the one which had enthralled her, along with all those other people, in that public setting.

'It's beautiful. I only saw it in daylight last time.'

'I knew a chap whose job was replacing broken light-bulbs on the Clifton Bridge. It was a full-time occupation, up a ladder all day and every day. Whenever he reached one end he had to go straight back to the beginning and start again. It drove him crazy. In the end, he gave up the whole thing and became a milkman.'

Erinna giggled. 'A variation on the Golden Gate syndrome?'

John knew a forced laugh from a real one. 'Are you very angry with me, Erinna?'

'Angry?' She stiffened up even further. 'Not exactly angry. I—I don't know how to describe what I feel.'

'I suspect anger comes into it somewhere.' John's gentleness only increased her confusion. 'I wouldn't blame you if it did. That was a dirty trick to play on you in a way, but I've never wanted anything so much as to see your face when the penny dropped.'

'See my face?' Erinna had been so busy dealing with the situation from her own angle, she'd given no thought to John's motives. 'But you couldn't see it from where you were!'

'That's what you think.' He pulled up, rather sharply, at some traffic lights. 'Must be roadworks,' he muttered. 'These aren't usually here.'

'You mean, you were watching me?' Erinna pressed.

'You bet I was. I enjoyed it enough on the way in, when you realised we were about to hear Devin O'Connor. But when you got the message, that he and I were one and the same man...'

'But I was right at the back of the room, and you were...'

'When I give a public reading, I can see each member of my audience, as an individual—which is what they are. I often pick out one or two to address, in my mind, although I don't show it. Your face was an absolute picture, Erinna. It was all I could do, not to rush right back to you and...'

'And what?'

John shrugged. 'And reassure you. You looked—stricken.'

'That's how I felt! Flabbergasted—and a mixture of other things as well...excited, upset...but at the same time it was as if I'd known. Always known the truth, in some part of me...'

This was so difficult, so delicate! How could she tell him the true depth and extent of her responses? Here, now, while they were on their way to—wherever they were on their way to?

'I wouldn't be a bit surprised,' John was saying.

'Surprised?'

'If you *did* suspect, at some level. That there was something not quite—shall we say obvious?—about me. Your intuition is a highly developed and perceptive organ, Miss Casey. That's one of the factors that make you such an outstanding student of literature, especially poetry.' He flashed her a quick grin.

'But, John, some of the things I've *said* to you!' she lamented. 'I feel such an idiot!'

'Well, please don't. There was no way in the world you could have guessed. In fact, when you said them, you were almost justified, Erinna. I have to keep that pragmatic front intact, I have to plaster it on, all the time I'm in company, up there at the University. I just can't risk anyone finding out. It means more to me than you could understand, keeping Devin separate from John. They're both equally real, living parts of me. Combined, I suppose they make the whole me, but it's more than my professional career's worth to get the two of them confused in anyone's mind. Including my own.'

'I do understand.' He was wrong; Erinna had rarely understood anything so completely. 'And has no one else ever cracked it? This—this front?'

'No one. You're a pioneer. Another first for Erinna Casey.'

'But *I* wouldn't have guessed, if you hadn't invited me here tonight. I might have grown more suspicious that there was something about you, something you weren't showing us, but...'

'That's fair enough. It was my decision to let you into the secret. Now I have to trust you to keep it to yourself.'

'I will, John.'

'I know you will.'

There was a silence while he slowed down to turn off the highway. Erinna peered out at a meandering country lane.

'I thought you said we were going to the suburbs?'

'Perhaps suburbs was misleading. It's a village—basically a dormitory for Bristol, but it likes to consider itself the genuine, picturesque, rural article.'

'I see. And that's where...' She had almost come out with it! Almost spat it out, at last!

But John was cutting in firmly. 'That's where we're going. I hope I can guarantee no more surprises this evening, Erinna. You've kept admirably cool so far—I'm sure you can carry on the good work now?'

Apparently a frivolous question, but she detected the serious note of appeal, even warning, underneath. Her stomach tightened, and her heart seemed to shrivel and droop. His message had struck its target—indirect, yet square to the centre.

'I won't let you down.' Given half a chance, I'd never let you down, John... 'Are we nearly there, then?'

'Three minutes. You must be tired.'

'So must you. You're the one who's been doing the real work.'

'There's work, and work, Erinna. I do this all the time, remember.'

'Do you? How often? I noticed the man said they were welcoming you *back...*'

'I do it somewhere nearly every week. Poetry is for the people, after all—for hearing, for sharing. It's an oral, not a written tradition. Not designed to be studied, set on exam papers, analysed, dissected. That's what Devin O'Connor believes, at least! He writes his stuff—feels it, plans it—to be read aloud, so he makes a point of going wherever he's invited, to recite or speak to clubs and groups all over the country. You'd be amazed how many there are and how often they hold meetings.'

Erinna was digesting the implications of this speech. 'Are you telling me this is your major commitment? This is where you go, when you go away at weekends?'

'That's what I'm telling you.'

'But not always here, in Bristol?'

'Good lord, no! This one happened to be here, that's all. I'm peripatetic, the original troubadour! I cover all points of the compass, including Ireland, of course. Last weekend I was in Leeds, and the one before that I think it was Ipswich, or was it Leicester? Recently I trekked all the way up to Edinburgh. That's why I'm not always at my sunniest, first thing Monday morning.'

'Then why are we . . .'

'Here we are!' It was a residential street with pleasant, modern detached houses. It could have been anywhere on the more affluent fringes of any English city, town or commuter village. If Erinna had been puzzled before, now she was utterly bewildered.

John drew up outside one of the houses and switched off the engine. 'OK?'

'Yes, but . . .'

He was out of the car, reaching in the back for their overnight bags. Erinna got out too, and waited on the pavement. Eyeing the house, with its invitingly lit downstairs windows, she struggled to control the trembling which was starting up all over her body.

John locked the car doors. 'Coming? It's after eleven-thirty; they'll be wondering where we've got to.'

'John . . .' She hung back, fighting a current of panic.

'Don't give up on me—or yourself—now, Erinna! It's all right, nothing to worry about, they're . . .'

'Johnny!' The front door was flung open and a female form stood on the threshold, arms outstretched, framed in welcoming light.

'Tricia!' John left Erinna, and strode up the path to the woman.

Erinna stood in that cold, dark, neat front garden, and watched the two figures as they met and embraced, then separated and held each other at arm's length, laughing and chattering in unison. She took in nothing of what they said, only registering this deep-rooted affection, years of old familiarity, a mutual satisfaction in meeting—all of it flowed from each of them, and out to Erinna, whose instincts received it, weeping.

To this person he was neither Dr Bryce nor Devin, not even John. He was Johnny, as intimate as anyone could be. If Erinna had not been a stranger in a bucolic backwater, in the middle of the night, she might have turned tail and fled. But she was stuck with this predicament and she would see it through, because that was how she...

'Erinna?' Now John was beckoning to her; then, when she still did not move, coming back towards her.

'Yes, I...' Erinna began to walk, slowly, a dreamlike glide.

'Come on in!' The woman's tone was mellow and relaxed. 'It's freezing out here. Come and get warm!'

'Sorry, I...' Their precious central heating would be escaping into the chilly night, and it was selfish of any guest to let that happen, so Erinna quickened her step.

The woman ushered her in and shut the door. Then she moved back to John, whose arm immediately went round her shoulders. Together, a unit, they smiled at Erinna across the cosy hall.

It was, as if there had been any doubt, the female in his photograph. Erinna would know her anywhere, that handsome face, the short dark hair, the intelligent grey eyes... anywhere. In fact, it was remarkably recognisable for a face seen just the once, on paper, under somewhat fraught circumstances...

'Erinna, meet Patricia. Tricia, this is Erinna Casey.'

'Lovely to meet you, Erinna.' Patricia was smiling and holding out her right hand. 'I've heard about you. John's star student, no less.'

'How do you do?' Erinna shook the hand as confidently as she could. So, John had been talking about her, doubtless regaling Patricia with the full comedy, so that they could share a chuckle at her expense.

'See the likeness?' John gave Patricia another squeeze.

'Likeness?' He couldn't know, surely, about the time she had been in his bedroom and seen the photo, as well as a lot more besides?

'To me, of course! This is Mrs Harrison, my favourite sister!'

'Your *only* sister,' Tricia interjected.

'*Sister!*'

They could see Erinna's jaw drop; but at least her stomach did its double somersault in private. 'But you said...'

'I said I had a baby sister. This is she.'

Suddenly, Erinna wasn't just smiling, but beaming—inanely, perhaps, but she had no choice. Turning to Patricia, she explained, 'He said his sister was the ultimate career woman, so I'm afraid I assumed...'

'Did he, indeed? Thanks, brother!'

'Well, she is!' John leapt to his own defence. 'Go on, Trish, you can't deny it. Just because you run a home and family with all the precision of a major-general, it doesn't mean you're not a professional. You've been set dead on course since you were fourteen, and to the best of my knowledge nothing's ever stood in your way. Not

Vic, or Kirsty and Joe... nothing. You've always said so.'

'Yes, but "career woman"? It makes me sound like one of those terrifying ladies who reject all personal temptations so as to pour their total energies into the job! I try to be a good all-rounder, and anyway, I couldn't do it without Vic, you know that, John.'

John was pointing an accusing finger at Erinna. '*You* jumped to conclusions, didn't you, Miss Casey? *You* presumed she must be singular and independent—that she couldn't be married as well as aspiring to the upper echelons of academic law? Your feminist prejudices are showing!'

'I admit it.' At this moment, Erinna would happily admit anything. 'That's exactly what I did think.' She hoped he would never know how much else she had presumed, and how misguidedly.

'These poets,' Tricia complained. 'They talk in code, that's the trouble. They provide the barest outline and expect us ordinary mortals to flesh out the rest. Don't you find that with John, or is he a different kettle of tea when he's being Big Chief Visiting Fellow?'

'He's different, certainly.' Erinna glanced at John before returning Tricia's smile.

'Did he explain about his pseudonym? I helped him to choose it, actually, years ago when he first went in for publication and decided to keep his two selves apart. Devin means dark poet, and Connor means high desire. Isn't that romantic?'

'Romantic, yes.' Erinna's gaze locked with John's, an ironic exchange.

'She did know that,' John told his sister. 'In fact I had no need to enlighten her, even if I'd wanted to. She was telling *me* what it meant, long before I had any intention of sharing the information.'

'You knew him as a poet, then?' Tricia was interested.

'I knew John, and I knew the works of Devin O'Connor. In no detail did I associate the two—until tonight.'

'You mean, when he took you to hear him read this evening, you didn't know it was going to be him?'

'I had no idea who I was going to hear, or where, or why. I most definitely did not expect it to be him.'

'Goodness, you must have had a shock!' Tricia might be a hard-headed exponent of the law, but she shared her brother's humanity.

'You could say that.' Erinna's eyes were on John again.

'He's wicked.' Tricia frowned at him fondly. 'Mind you, he'll have had his reasons. John always has his reasons.'

'I did.' John leaned on the stair-rails, hands in pockets. 'Don't waste any anxiety over Erinna. She'll survive.'

'I think I understand his reasons,' Erinna assured Tricia.

'Most of them,' John agreed. 'I'll make sure she understands all of them eventually.' It was a cryptic, throw-away remark to his sister.

Tricia nodded thoughtfully, then sprang into action. 'What am I *doing*, keeping you standing around out here when you must be exhausted? I'm so sorry, Erinna. It's the excitement of seeing John after several months—and meeting you, of course. Please do come and have some refreshment, or would you prefer to collapse straight into bed?'

While Erinna groped for a suitable reply, John was marching into the living-room, announcing over his shoulder, 'What Erinna and I would like is a cup of tea. Wouldn't we, Erinna?'

'As it happens, yes, I would.'

'Right. You go in there with John and I'll be back with a pot for us all in a minute. Sit down. Make yourselves at home. Do you like Earl Grey? Oh, and by the way, Vic sends his apologies. He's been at the word processor all day and he couldn't prop his eyes open any longer. He retired to bed an hour ago, but he'll see you in the morning.'

She disappeared down the corridor to the kitchen, and Erinna followed John into a comfortable family lounge. John sank at once into a plush armchair, resting his head back and closing his eyes.

Sitting opposite him, Erinna seized the opportunity to take a long, lingering look at his face. When he opened his eyes, without warning, she didn't even bother to pretend she hadn't been staring at him.

He smiled lazily across at her. 'OK now?'

She nodded.

'No more shocks, Erinna, I promise.'

'How do you know?'

He frowned. 'How do you mean, how do I know?'

'You might not have any more lined up for me. You can't be sure I won't have any for *you*.'

'Hmmm.' He shut his eyes again. 'I'm not even going to try and work out the hidden ciphers in that one!'

'Nor am I.' They shared a smile, then Erinna grew solemn. 'John?'

'Yes, Erinna?'

'Why didn't you tell me we were staying at your sister's? I can understand you keeping all the rest a secret, but I don't see why...'

He ran a hand through his hair. 'I suppose I wanted to make this whole event unfold for you, in its own time, in its own way. Giving selected highlights away at the beginning would have spoilt it for me, and I suppose I thought for you, too. Anyway, I've already told you, I hate anyone to know too much about me, the real me, till I feel good and ready that they should.'

'All the same, I wish you had. Not the rest, just this.'

'I'm sorry if it caused you undue suspense.' But there was a gleam, a satisfaction, in his smile. Erinna decided not to pursue this tack—not yet, at any rate. Maybe one day, when she was less tired, and more sure of her ground... 'Kirsty and Joe.' John was pointing at another of those framed photographs on the mantelpiece. The same two children of course—not unlike their mother, in feature and expression, and not unlike John either, unsurprisingly, since they were... 'My niece and nephew. Gorgeous kids. You'll meet them tomorrow. Rather too early tomorrow, for my taste, if I know anything about Kirsty and Joe.'

'How old are they?'

'I'm not sure. I lose count.' He waved a vague hand, every inch the bachelor uncle. 'Four, six, thereabouts? Kirsty's older, I know that much.'

'Obviously.' Erinna, an expert in the field with all those sisters and brothers, got up to take a closer look at the picture. 'I'd say she's seven and he's five.'

'Joe's just turned six,' Tricia confirmed, entering the room at this strategic point, 'and Kirsty will be eight in June.' She set the tea tray down. 'I've brought some of Vic's shortbread, in case you're peckish.'

'Peckish is what I am.' John stretched his whole body luxuriously.

'But we had that huge meal!' Erinna protested. All the same, the shortbread was enticingly golden-brown on its plate.

'That was hours ago. I've burned up a lot of fuel since then.' He leaned over and took two chunks of it.

'He always was greedy. I can't think how he stays so slim,' Tricia grumbled.

'I jog,' John reminded her, through a crunchy mouthful.

'So you do. Still keeping it up, is he?'

'Oh, yes, he keeps it up.' Erinna nibbled a piece of shortbread. 'His progress round the lake is one of the regular features of campus life. People set their watches by it.'

'Even in all that snow we had?' Tricia was pouring tea into three cups.

'Especially in all that snow.' Erinna's voice was steady, but she couldn't risk meeting John's eye.

'It takes more than a few snowdrifts—or low-flying snowballs—to deter *me*.'

John was staring at her, she sensed it. She also sensed that he was grinning. In search of a safer subject, she turned to Tricia. 'Did you say your husband had been at the word processor all day?'

'That's right. He's another of these creative writers. This family's riddled with them, heaven help us.'

'Not a poet?'

'Not in John's sense, no. He's a novelist.' Tricia handed out the cups of tea.

'Really? Are they published? Would I have read any?'

'That depends on whether you're a science fiction buff.'

'Erinna's more into romance,' John volunteered, sipping his tea.

Now Erinna did confront him. 'I do like science fiction, when it's not too way out. After all, it's the essence of fantasy, isn't it?'

'Oh, Vic's is quality stuff—you'd like Vic's. He's doing really well, isn't he, Trish?'

'They certainly sell. It's very convenient for me,' she explained to Erinna, 'because it suits him to write from early morning till tea time. Then he gets some exercise, collecting the children, and he makes supper for us all. He's more in charge around here than I am, really. We used to have an *au pair*, but we don't need one any more now that Joe's at school full-time. I've got some wonderful neighbours who help in emergencies and holidays.'

'Genuine teamwork.' John nodded approvingly.

'I think that's marvellous!' Erinna was wistful, thinking of her own mother, and how different things might have been, if only...

'Yes, we're very lucky. And very organised, mind you. As John said, I'd never let anything stand between me and my profession. I'd never have missed having children, but if I'd had to hire a permanent nanny or housekeeper, that's what I'd have done.'

Erinna was glimpsing the true grit beneath Tricia's affable exterior. This brother and sister had much in common, but they were like inside-out versions of one another. The woman had chosen to present her soft, feminine side to the world, guarding her tough single-mindedness within.

'I look forward to meeting the children.' Erinna stifled a yawn.

'You're wiped out, and it's terribly late!' Tricia was sympathetic. 'Come on, drink up, and I'll show you where you're sleeping. We've only got the one spare room, so Johnny's on the settee down here.'

'I—well, if that's OK...' Erinna could only hope she wasn't blushing. Here was the last uncertainty, resolved, just like that; and here, too, was that see-saw of regret and relief, mercilessly rocking her.

Tricia had evidently noticed nothing. 'Oh, he won't mind, will you, big brother? He sleeps wherever he drops; always did.'

'Right. I'll be out like a light, wherever you put me. No problem.'

Erinna turned sharply away, seeking physical escape from that persistent, penetrating mental image. At the same time, she knew she never would escape it, wherever she turned, however she tried.

'The only thing I mind,' John was continuing, 'is when your brats descend and use me as a trampoline at the crack of dawn. Couldn't you lock them in their quarters, or something?'

'I most certainly could not. What a suggestion!' Tricia was escorting Erinna to the door. 'Anyway, you love it. Don't listen to him, Erinna. He loves every moment of it.'

'I believe you.' Erinna felt drained, but peculiarly calm, now that particular tension was released, now she knew it had been taken for granted that she and John would occupy separate rooms. A house full of chaperons, just as he'd promised.

It was no real resolution, of course. There was still that profound uncertainty; more than ever, in fact, now she found herself in this state of limbo—knowing so much about him, and yet knowing nothing about her place in his life, present or future.

'I'll just show Erinna where everything is,' Tricia called, leading the way through the hall, 'then I'll be back with your sleeping-bag.'

'Fine.' John stayed sprawled in his chair. Erinna could feel his gaze, acute on her back, and knew it was quizzical.

At the door, she swung round to meet it. 'Goodnight then, John!'

''Night, Erinna. You'll be all right now, won't you?'

'Of course she will!' Tricia was waiting patiently at the foot of the stairs. 'Our spare bed's very comfortable.'

'I'll be fine,' Erinna said, but she was looking at John. 'Thanks.' She gave a slight shrug, as if no words in her vocabulary were adequate.

'Thank *you*.' He hesitated. As she turned to leave, he added, 'How about exploring the area tomorrow? The Mendips are spectacular, even at this time of year.'

'But haven't we got to get back?'

Tricia had grown tired of waiting, and now returned to the doorway behind Erinna. 'I told John—didn't he tell you? Honestly, men! They're hopeless! I told him we have to go away in the morning. We're pledged to visit Vic's mother in Cornwall, till Sunday night. But you're welcome to stay on here as long as you like. In fact, you can make yourselves useful, feeding Joe's guinea pigs.' She shook her head at her brother, reproachful. 'You're impossible, you really are! Poor Erinna, how could she even pack the right things if you didn't put her properly in the picture?'

'Erinna knows why I didn't put her properly in the picture.' John was staring at Erinna, intently now. 'As for packing the right things, I'm sure you can lend her an extra sweater and some wellies and an old coat, if necessary. Can't we live life as it comes, step by step?'

'I know that's always been your philosophy. Fine as long as no one else depends on your next step.' Tricia was sharp, under the mild observation. Then her voice softened. 'Come and get some rest, Erinna.'

'Sleep well, then!' John's smile was direct and unashamed.

'You too, John.'

Yet another little irony: it was her turn to take the conventional bed, leaving him tucked up on a sofa.

Erinna was meditative as she followed her hostess up the stairs.

CHAPTER TEN

ERINNA'S watch told her it was just after seven when she was rudely awoken by very young, very shrill voices on the other side of her door.

'It's a *stupid* picture,' one of them was squeaking. 'Cows aren't that colour or that shape. It looks more like a—a caterpillar or a *worm...*'

'How can it be a worm? Worms don't have legs! And cows *can* be this colour! There's a whole field full of brown ones just like this, on the way to school!'

'OK, then, why is it so long? Cows aren't long, they're more sort of square. And their legs don't go down the middle, they have one at each corner.'

'Cows have to be long because they have four stomachs,' the artist asserted.

'*Four stomachs?* Don't be crazy! How could they have four?'

'They need four because they eat grass and it has to be turned into milk. It's like a kind of—kind of factory.'

'I don't believe you. You're making it up,' the critic accused.

'I'm *not*!' If Erinna guessed right, this was little Joe, and he was on the verge of self-righteous tears. 'Miss Baker said, and that was why we had to draw a cow.'

'Well, even if it's true they have four stomachs, they wouldn't be arranged in a long line like that. Anyway, where's its udder?'

'Its other what?'

'Its *udder*, silly!' The elder sister was blinding him with science. 'Where the milk comes out from! You haven't even *drawn* an udder. No wonder it looks more like a...'

'Kirsty! Joe!' A door opening on to the landing, and the timely interference of an adult male voice. 'Do you have to conduct your zoological debates out here, at this hour? For God's sake, go back in your bedroom, or down to the kitchen and get some milk if you must— but quietly! Have you forgotten there's a visitor in the spare room?'

'A visitor? Who?' The childish treble gave way to an equally piercing whisper.

'The lady who's here with Uncle John, of course. I *told* you...'

'Uncle John! Uncle Johnny's here!'

'You knew perfectly well he was coming late last night. Now he's asleep on the settee, so don't go barging in there and...'

'Uncle Johnny, on the settee! Yay! Whee!'

Four small feet thumped down the stairs, two small bodies hurtled across the hall. Erinna had never met Vic, but she could imagine his resigned, sleepy shrug as he retreated behind his own door, and climbed gratefully back into bed beside his warm wife.

Erinna stretched voluptuously, the full width of this double bed which she had all to herself. Then she lay and inspected the neat, tasteful décor which she had been too weary to take in last night.

From downstairs floated noises of bouncing and bundling, punctuated with high-pitched screams of joy and avuncular protestations. Erinna grinned with more satisfaction than compassion, then she sighed contentedly and rolled over in search of another hour's much-needed rest.

*   *   *

About twelve hours later, she sat with John on that same sofa, now restored to its proper order. The curtains were drawn against another murky February evening, and an aromatic wood-fire flickered in the grate. The house was silent after this morning's rampagings, then the chaos while the Harrison tribe had sorted themselves out and hit the road. Now it belonged, temporarily, to Erinna and John, settling into a sympathetic peace around them.

'Another cup?' John waved a hospitable hand at the coffee-pot.

'No, thanks.' Erinna leaned back on the cushions. 'It was a grand meal, John. I was famished! Must have been all that fresh air and exercise. How long have you numbered cooking among your many skills?'

'I've always enjoyed it, but I can't be bothered much, just for myself. Yes, I suppose I'm quite good at it, in an eclectic, self-taught kind of way. You need an appreciative audience really. Vic's rather keen on it, too, but he's got the family to make it worth while.'

'Have you never gone in much for the domestic scene?' The most probing question of all, and she asked it in the most offhand way.

'I've tended to keep myself to myself,' he replied, tersely.

After a brief pause, Erinna chose the safer topic. 'I wish *I* was any use in the kitchen. It was never my strongest point. Two of my sisters are far better at it than I'll ever be.'

'No one can be good at everything, not even you!' John smiled. 'And as I say, someone has to be the grateful public, savouring the results!'

'Oh, when it comes to the eating part, I'm up there among the experts. Especially after a day like this.' Erinna yawned. 'Do you make a habit of striding about rugged hillsides, or was it all part of this endurance test you're putting me through?'

'If I find myself within easy reach of a rugged hillside, I do like to make use of it.' John was gazing at her. 'Is that how you see this weekend, Erinna? An endurance test?'

'Not really. A test of something, maybe...' But tonight she was only aware of this sense of deep well-being, this pleasantly physical tiredness, totally without stress.

'Have I dragged you too far? Pushed you too hard, yet again?'

'Not at all! I can take it. To tell you the truth, I loved it.'

He studied her flushed cheeks and bright eyes. 'You look as if you did, I must say. You should do it more often.'

'I'd like to.'

'There's plenty of fine countryside around Mid-Anglia. We'll creep furtively away and go for Wordsworthian rambles in it, shall we?'

'You mean, between your poetry expeditions and our rehearsals and tutorials and seminars and lectures, not to mention the comprehensive revision programme I'm about to embark on...'

John was watching her. 'You're really thinking we can't afford to let any of our respective colleagues see us and start any scandal buzzing, aren't you?'

'I—I imagine that's what *you'd* be thinking, John. It wouldn't exactly be in character, after all—suddenly striking off into the hills in the company of one of your own Finalists? You, of all people!'

There was an extended, uncomfortable pause. Then, in one quick movement, John slid along the sofa until he was close to her, swivelling so that he could look directly into her face. His knees brushed hers, but otherwise he made no move to touch her. 'Erinna...'

'What?'

'If rumours did circulate about us, would there be any truth in them?'

'That depends on the rumours,' she pointed out with cautious logic, though her pulse was racing.

'If people reckoned we were...involved...rather more deeply than your average student and tutor...' He weighed each word; his tone was intense, but dry. 'If they guessed that we felt something...rather stronger than the plain mutual respect frequently generated in a successful intellectual rapport...'

'Oh, John!' Crazily, Erinna erupted in peals of laughter. 'Don't be such a—such an *academic*!'

'But I *am* an academic, Erinna.'

'Only half of you. What about the other half? So, we've heard what Dr Bryce has to say. Couldn't you give Devin a chance?'

For several seconds, John stared into the middle distance. Then he turned abruptly back to face her, seized both her hands and gazed into her eyes. When he spoke, it was in the husky tones of a passionate poet.

'You know full well what Devin would say, Erinna— brave, beautiful, *peaceful* Erinna Casey! He'd say he adored you with all his heart and soul and strength and might. He'd say that if he didn't tell you now—shout it from the rooftops—get it off his chest at last, he was in real danger of dissolving, or exploding into a million fragments. If he didn't speak his heart to you now, he'd never speak to anyone again! He'd say he loved you from the first day he saw you, and no matter how many guided missiles you hurl at him—verbal or otherwise—he'll only come back for more. He'd say you've bewitched him, and he'd be blessing you and cursing you in all the poetic imagery he could lay his tongue on, because you're the most glorious, and the most infuriating thing that's entered his arid life for too many long years.'

He finally broke off there, his voice cracking, but losing none of its force.

'John...' Erinna's heart was singing, so why was she whispering? 'Only Devin? Only Devin would say all that?'

'Devin would mean every syllable of it.' His grasp on her hands was so tight, she could feel the nails digging into her palms.

'And John? What about John?'

His grip loosened, and his expression changed to something more considered. Just as Erinna's heart began to sink again, he released her hands, and gathered her into his arms instead.

'John seems to favour action, rather than speeches, when it comes to the crunch.' As if to prove it, those were almost his final words before his actions overtook them. 'John knows what he really wants—*who* he wants—*how* he wants her—but telling her so—isn't as easy—as showing her...'

The mutters became murmurs, then no more than vague breaths in her ear. Then they died away altogether, leaving a rich, pulsating silence.

It had simmered too long, this tension between them, and now it boiled over. The heat was scorching, but it was cleansing, too—a purification, a cauterisation of all those raw emotional nerve-endings. Neither wisdom nor reason had any part in this union. Both were banished, so that only sensation remained.

John demanded, and Erinna gladly gave. He demanded her response, with his hands, his mouth, all his body. He demanded access to every smooth, white inch of her, and she willingly granted it. Then he explored and worshipped, minutely, each fold, curve and cranny of her, taking his time until she was nothing but a mass of longing, until at last she was vibrantly alive, all over, from the flesh inwards.

Her hands ranged freely too, discovering places where her gaze had already trespassed. Asleep, unconscious, he had been potent enough. Wide awake he was the life force that inspired the universe, he was every surge of power she had ever imagined, and a hundred more she had hardly dreamed of. Her own strength depended on his, filling her full, fulfilling her. This claim he made on her now was all she had ever wanted, and she wanted it from him... at this instant... desperately.

She cried out aloud, as he entered her. Pleasure and pain tangled in the cry, but did it matter which was which, or in what proportion? Gradually the pain ebbed and the pleasure flowed, and there was only pure delight: an anticipation, an exhilaration like no other in human experience. Rising to a suffusion—a tense peak—then a cascading release, like no other in human experience. The centre, the core—Erinna understood in that endless, shattering moment—of all human experience.

Afterwards, there was this unbelievable stillness, a serenity beyond her fantasies, as they lay entwined on the soft hearthrug, their naked skins caressed by the glow from dying elm embers.

At long last, John stirred, extricated himself from Erinna with great reluctance, and reached over to throw a couple of logs on the fire.

'I know how it feels.' He came back to her arms.

'How what feels?'

'The fire. It was burning low, but now I've given it something to get its teeth into, it'll flare up again. And, with minimum encouragement, so will I.' He nibbled her ear, then buried his face in the tawny depths of her spreading hair.

But Erinna levered him away, to look into his face. 'Is this Devin I'm being introduced to? This—this poet-in-action? Or is it John?'

He mused. 'Both—yes, both. I can't feel the join. I think we have a successful fusion here, Miss Casey. I think we have lift-off!'

He was about to offer tangible proof, when she pushed him away again. This time, what she had to say was less simple. 'I love you. You do know that, don't you?'

'Which one of us? The Bryce, or the O'Connor?'

'Haven't you just told me we have fusion?'

John's face was circumspect, but Devin's radiance shone through. 'You haven't known Devin long. Don't forget, plain old John saw you first, and loved you first. He may not be so expressive, or so fluent, but his feelings might go deeper, and last longer...'

Erinna smiled up at him. 'I loved Devin, when he was words on a page. And the images behind the words, the feelings the words made me have. But I loved John when he was a man. One I could see and hear and—and touch; a man, real and three-dimensional, who irritated me, threatened me, alienated me, and taught me who and what I am.' Now she pulled him down to her again, winding her arms round him. 'I love you, John Bryce.' It felt superb, just saying it. 'I love you, and I want you. I've always wanted you. I'll always want you.'

But this time it was his turn to draw away. 'Erinna?'

'What is it?' She ached to feel him again, the whole of him, but she was alerted to his note of command, perhaps even warning.

'I've got to tell you something about myself. I've got to tell you now.'

She shifted to lie on her side, propped on one elbow, to see him better. 'So, tell me now.' Registering his face, she added, 'We've got all night.'

'I've never been married...' he began, diffidently.

'So I guessed—eventually.' She was sardonically encouraging.

'But years ago, when I was—oh, much about your age, I fell in love.'

Erinna nodded. This was scarcely surprising, after all. He was bound to have had his share of emotional experiments, a man like him...

'I fell in love, for the first and only other time in my life.'

This was a bit more unexpected, and Erinna sensed how crucial it was for him—and how difficult. 'Tell me about it,' she urged.

'She was twelve years older than me. I was a postgrad student, fresh from the production line. She was one of my tutors, a specialist on Chaucer, as a matter of fact. I remember, we were studying *The Romance of the Rose*. Anyway, she was married—happily enough, up till then. She had three kids, would you believe! So, you can see now why I felt a certain—shall we say sympathy?—with Anthony and Lindsay, in their passionate predicament...'

'Good lord, yes! How extraordinary!' At this moment, the tale he was telling seemed more real, more recent to Erinna than that other incident he had just dredged up. But she felt this twinge of amazement, even a peculiar satisfaction, at the way events fell into a pattern. This strange symmetry of things. 'And did she feel the same about you, John?'

'So she led me to believe. We had a fling—an intense affair.'

'Poor woman!' Erinna's imaginative sympathy went out to anyone trapped in such a conflict, struggling against so many social conventions.

'Poor woman—foolish woman—who's to say?' John could be philosophical now, but she was only too aware of the sufferings it must have caused, all those years ago, when he had been just her age, and the woman had been just *his* age now. 'Of course our meetings had to be conducted discreetly, but it lasted for months. I was obsessed with her—besotted. She was so mature, so *womanly*, compared to the callow girls I knew—or so it seemed to me then. Of course, I know better now.' He grinned, catching Erinna's expression.

'I'm not jealous, John.' Was it true? Was it even important? 'I want to know what happened, in the end.'

'In the end we were found out—inevitably, I suppose. There never could have been a real future in it, anyway. I don't think she'd have left her husband and family. I was finishing my MA, so I simply sat my final papers and left. But she...things were stricter, less flexible, even that short time ago. Attitudes were rigid, especially to women, and...it was grossly unfair, but rules were rules, and she was sacked. Or, to be more accurate, she was quietly pressurised to resign.'

'Oh, dear!' Erinna's compassion was genuine. She was also aware of a whole new dimension of understanding for John—growing by the minute.

'She had to give up that post because of me, Erinna, and she was so brilliant at it. It was a sin—a waste—a pitiful shame.'

'Did she ever get another?'

'I've no idea. She patched things up with her husband, and they moved away. I never heard from her, or even of her, again. It took me years to recover, and even then I went on blaming myself...'

'You've carried this guilt with you ever since.' Erinna felt so much for him at that moment, it hurt. 'You decided, if there was one mistake you'd never make again, it was that one. Of course.'

John relaxed now—now the worst was out—reaching to touch her cheek. 'I've had close female friends. I've had mild flirtations, would-be lovers...but I've never stayed in one spot long enough to let them develop. I've always held myself aloof, from other staff even, but especially from students. I've deliberately kept on the move, avoiding putting down roots. I've never let anyone far into my heart, or my life. It was such a traumatic start to my emotional experience, I just could not risk a repeat. So, now, here I am—older, wiser, but only marginally less chaste than you!'

Now he really had amazed her. 'You mean, in all those years, you've...'

'I tell you, I've lurked inside my shell. Oh, the urges are all intact, painfully present and correct—don't doubt that, for a second! But I've exercised self-discipline. Self-control...' He was deeply wry now. 'Yes, I've been celibate. So now, my lovely girl, I've got a lot of catching up to do, and you're the one I'm intending to do it with...'

His words were spent, and Erinna couldn't find any, either. She reached up to embrace him tenderly, as if he must need reassurance. At last she murmured, 'I'd never have guessed, John. You're—you're magnificent! You're...no woman could want a better—a more perfect start to *her* emotional experience...her female life...'

She burrowed into his shoulder, reddening, breathless at this revelation, and her own poignant reactions to it. John was trembling; was he crying? No, he was *laughing*! But when she stared into his eyes, they were alight with affection.

'Erinna, you're the sweetest creature in the world, underneath all the barbed Celtic wit! It's OK—I got plenty of practice in, before I decided to wait for Ms Right. Just a temporary retirement from the lists. I don't regret it, and I don't nurse any secret anxieties about my performance!' He was grinning broadly. 'Doing what comes naturally *does* come naturally, when the feelings are valid—eh, Miss Casey?'

'So I'm beginning to realise, Dr Bryce.'

'You were well worth the wait, Ms Right.'

'And so were you.' She pulled him close again.

But he had more to say. 'Now I'll tell you what, Erinna. Please treat me gently, because I'm about to spread my dreams under your feet.'

'I'll tread softly, don't worry. I'll always cherish your dreams.'

'Will you come to America with me? When you've got your First, and I've signed off my Fellowship? Come live with me and be my love—my wife—my better half. Come and share a new outlook in civilised New England. You can do a whole series of higher degrees, or teach, or run a bar, or drive a bus, or whatever the hell you like, as long as you do it around me!'

'Or raise a family?'

'That, too, if you can fit it into this heavy schedule. A shower of little Erinnas. As many as you like.'

'And little Johns, and Devins. After all, you're a marvel with kids.'

'How do you know that?'

'I heard you, early this morning. It was heart-warming. If some of your poor, cowed students could have witnessed you in action then...'

'That was neither Devin nor Dr Bryce. That was Uncle John.'

'Well, I love him as much as the others, so you needn't fret. Your secret is safe with me.'

He grew solemn. 'We really will have to keep the whole thing quiet, until after your exams, and after the play, too. Do you think you can handle our tutorials, or should I find some excuse to transfer you?'

'I can handle them, if you can. I'm not sacrificing my sessions with the brilliant Bryce, just on account of some minor sentimental upheaval. But if *you*'re afraid you'll find it too daunting...'

'I am not. John Bryce is the original iron man, you know that. As long as I can keep the volatile O'Connor under control...he's not half so practised at masking his baser desires.'

'Tell him we'll get away at weekends,' Erinna promised. 'And if there are frustrations, we'll have all the more fun making up for them when we cross the water—I mean the pond—together. Of course I'll come to the States with you, John. It's a fabulous idea. And what's more, here's another pledge. I'll give you the most stunning Beatrice you've ever seen. It'll be all for you. It already was, anyway.' Even as she expressed it, she recognised another hidden truth.

'Your Beatrice has been stunning all along, as I knew it would be. Why do you think I was so chary about taking the wretched play on, when you first asked me? The very *thought* of you in that role left me with palpitations! I didn't think I could trust myself. Then I decided I must be made of sterner stuff, so I accepted your challenge.'

'And has it been as dreadful as you feared?' She crept closer to him now, and began raining tiny kisses on his face.

'Every bit as dreadful. Every bit. Sheer hell.'

'All that stupid business about Anthony—you must have been so furious with me!'

'I was sorry for you, mainly. I wanted to help...'

'Don't let's talk about that any more,' she implored between kisses. 'I had it coming—it was one of those lessons...if it hadn't been that, it would have been—something else—equally ridiculous...' The kisses reached his mouth, and melted against it. 'I'm a grown woman now, and I know what I want...who I want. I want Dr Bryce, and Uncle Johnny, and Devin...all of them, for ever, and all at once. Now.'

'You're not just brazen, you're plain greedy!' He rolled over on top of her, pinning her down. 'And where does John fit in among this lot?'

'John?' Her eyes sparkled. 'He knows exactly where he fits in. He fits in perfectly. He also knows those others—those private fantasies—have their parts to play; but he's *real*. He knows,' Erinna whispered, before her words evaporated into a rising, yearning passion, 'that he's the one I want most of all.'

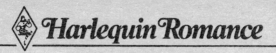
✦ Harlequin Romance

Coming Next Month

#2965 NO GREATER JOY Rosemary Carter
Alison fights hard against her attraction to Clint, driven by
bitter memories of a past betrayal. However, handsome,
confident, wealthy Clint Demaine isn't a man to take no for
an answer.

#2966 A BUSINESS ARRANGEMENT Kate Denton
When Lauren advertises for a husband interested in a businesslike approach to marriage, she doesn't expect a proposal from a
handsome Dallas attorney. If only love were part of the
bargain....

#2967 THE LATIMORE BRIDE Emma Goldrick
Mattie Latimore expects problems—supervising a lengthy
engineering project in the Sudan is going to be a daunting
experience. Yet heat, desert and hostile African tribes are
nothing compared to the challenge of Ryan Quinn. (More about
the Latimore family introduced in THE ROAD and TEMPERED
BY FIRE.)

#2968 MODEL FOR LOVE Rosemary Hammond
Felicia doesn't want to get involved with handsome financial
wizard Adam St. John—he reminds her of the man who once
broke her heart. So she's leery of asking him to let her sculpt
him—it might just be playing with fire!

#2969 CENTREFOLD Valerie Parv
Helping her twin sister out of a tight spot seems no big deal to
Danni—until she learns she's supposed to deceive
Rowan Traynor, her sister's boyfriend. When he discovers the
switch his reaction is a complete surprise to Danni....

#2970 THAT DEAR PERFECTION Alison York
A half share in a Welsh perfume factory is a far cry from Sophie's
usual job as a model, but she looks on it as an exciting
challenge. It is unfortunate that Ben Ross, her new partner,
looks on Sophie as a gold digger.

Available in March wherever paperback books are sold, or
through Harlequin Reader Service:

In the U.S.
901 Fuhrmann Blvd.
P.O. Box 1397
Buffalo, N.Y. 14240-1397

In Canada
P.O. Box 603
Fort Erie, Ontario
L2A 5X3

Keepsake

Harlequin Books

You're never too young to enjoy romance. Harlequin for you . . . and Keepsake, young-adult romances destined to win hearts, for your daughter.

Pick one up today and start your daughter on her journey into the wonderful world of romance.

Two new titles to choose from each month.

Worldwide Library provides the best in historical
romance—magnificent sagas of passion, romance,
adventure and suspense set during some of the most
turbulent and dazzling periods in history.

		Quantity
CLASH BY NIGHT—Doreen Owens Malek Set against the drama of World War II France, a story of passionate dreams and undying patriotism.	$4.50	☐
SEASON OF LOVING—Shirley Larson Wealth, power and privilege—he possessed everything—except the woman he desired and the son he loved more than life itself.	$3.95	☐
SCANDALOUS SPIRITS—Erin Yorke Set during the Roaring Twenties, a young woman running from unspeakable danger finds adventure and passion in the arms of a reckless stranger.	$4.50	☐
THURSDAY AND THE LADY—Patricia Matthews A story of a proud and passionate love set during America's most unforgettable era—as suffragettes waged their struggle for the vote, the gold rush spurred glorious optimism and the Civil War loomed on the horizon.	$4.50	☐

Total Amount	$ _____
Plus 75¢ Postage	.75
Payment enclosed	_____

Please send a check or money order payable to Worldwide Library.

In the U.S.A.	In Canada
Worldwide Library 901 Fuhrmann Blvd. Box 1325 Buffalo, NY 14269-1325	Worldwide Library P.O. Box 609 Fort Erie, Ontario L2A 5X3

Please Print

Name: _____

Address: _____

City: _____

State/Prov: _____

Zip/Postal Code: _____

 WORLDWIDE LIBRARY

HSR-1

Worldwide Library provides the best in historical romance—magnificent sagas of passion, romance, adventure, and suspense set during some of the most turbulent and dazzling periods in history.

		Quantity
SPRING WILL COME—Sherry DeBorde A young Southern woman is left alone to face overwhelming odds during the tumultuous years leading up to and including the Civil War.	$3.95	[ ]
THE BARGAIN—Veronica Sattler A young woman accepts a position as "governess" to the Duke's grandson but discovers that he is not a small child but a handsome young man.	$4.50	☐
UNTIL I RETURN—Laura Simon A novel of love and adventure in nineteenth- century Nantucket.	$3.95	☐
DEFY THE EAGLE—Lynn Bartlett An enthralling saga of love set during the dramatic period of the Roman Empire in Britain.	$4.95	☐

Total Amount	$	
Plus 75¢ Postage		.75
Payment enclosed